BABYSITTING NIGHTMARES

THE VAMPIRE DOLL

KAT SHEPHERD

ILLUSTRATED BY RAYANNE VIEIRA

[Imprint]
MAKE YOUR MARK

New York

[Imprint]
MAKE YOUR MARK

A part of Macmillan Publishing Group, LLC
120 Broadway, New York, NY 10271

Library of Congress Cataloging-in-Publication Data is available.

ISBN 978-1-250-15703-4 (hardcover) / ISBN 978-1-250-15704-1 (ebook)

Our books may be purchased in bulk for promotional, educational, or business use. Please contact your local bookseller or the Macmillan Corporate and Premium Sales Department at (800) 221-7945 ext. 5442 or by email at MacmillanSpecialMarkets@macmillan.com.

Book design by Eileen Savage

Imprint logo designed by Amanda Spielman

Illustrations by Rayanne Vieira

First edition, 2020

1 3 5 7 9 10 8 6 4 2

mackids.com

Stealing this? Advise against.
Unless you wish to know the angst
Of tiny watchers, ever watching
Evil plotters, ever hatching
Furtive whispers late at night
Darting shadows, full of spite
Pitter-patters down your halls
Your life forever plagued by dolls.

THIS BOOK IS FOR OLD FRIENDS.
HOW CHERISHED YOU ARE, DEAR ONES!
HOW VERY LOVED YOU ARE.

PROLOGUE

THE KITCHEN WAS dark except for the tarnished brass lamp that hung over the simple wooden table where an old woman bent over an old-fashioned high chair. She picked up a baby spoon and dipped it into a bowl on the high chair's tray, making a coaxing sound in her throat like a mother bird.

"That's right, eat up," the old woman said. "I found it especially for you, because I know it's your favorite." She chuckled and picked up a soft cloth napkin from the table beside her. "Messy baby," she scolded playfully. When she put the napkin down, it was blotted with bright red streaks.

The little spoon clinked in the bowl again, and as the gnarled hand inched forward, the spoon's ornate handle caught the light, revealing a delicate owl filigreed at the top. There was a sound like a cat lapping at a bowl of milk, and the crone chuckled again. "Now mind your manners, little miss! No slurping at the table!" She dabbed again with the napkin, and more crimson blots bloomed on the snowy linen.

Soon the spoon rattled in the empty bowl, and when the old woman placed the napkin on the table for the final time, it was soaked through with red. She stood, her bony legs poking out beneath the ruffled hem of her nightgown like two dead branches. Her bare feet shuffled across the worn wooden floor as she walked away from the little figure in the high chair.

It was a china doll. Fat sausage curls framed the heart-shaped face with its first-blush cheeks and limpid, painted-on eyes. The rosy lips were slightly parted, as though the doll had paused in mid-sentence. Thin, red rivulets oozed down the creamy white chin, soiling the snowy lace bib fastened at the neck.

The old woman sang to herself as she washed up, water swirling pink down the drain. Suddenly she paused. "What was that, Mary Rose?" She looked at the doll and giggled. "Still hungry? My, oh, my! You certainly are a growing girl!" She turned back to the sink and called over her shoulder. "Don't worry, my sweet. I'll have more for you tomorrow." Her tuneless singing resumed, the crooked melody hanging in the dim, yellow light of the room.

In the high chair, the doll's painted blue eyes stared lifelessly at the wall.

Then they blinked.

The doll turned her head, and a tiny tongue snaked out and licked the last red drops from the cold porcelain lips.

CHAPTER
1

TANYA MARTINEZ FOLDED her tawny arms and leaned back, resting her head against the wall. "Dare," she said confidently. Her brown eyes were steady as she watched her three best friends huddle together to plan. "And make it a good one this time," she added. "No more *I dare you to eat a hot dog* and junk like that."

"Don't look at me," Rebecca Chin answered. She brushed her russet bangs off her forehead. "Maggie's the one who threw that into the mix."

Maggie Anderson rolled her eyes. "I took it back! It's not like you actually had to *do* it." She looked down and picked at the cuticles around her short, glitter-painted nails. "How was I supposed to know you were that serious about being a vegetarian?"

"Oh, I don't know, maybe because I stopped eating animals when I was *four*?" Tanya shot back. "Honestly, Mags, we've been friends since preschool. Haven't you been paying attention?"

Maggie flopped back onto her sleeping bag. "Not really," she said, her voice playful. "I only pay attention to myself." The others laughed, and Tanya tossed a pillow at Maggie, who squealed in protest.

Clio Carter-Peterson stood up and stretched, her slender brown arms reaching for the ceiling. "Okay, so no food-related dares allowed. That works for me. I'm not about to eat some vanilla-and-hot-sauce sundae again."

"Hey!" Maggie protested. "That actually turned out pretty good!"

Clio laughed. "Says you." Her hazel eyes sparkled beneath her thick lashes. "Oh. I just thought of a great idea for a dare!" She gestured to Rebecca and Maggie, and the three bent their heads together, their whispers just muffled enough that Tanya couldn't quite make out the words.

Maggie let out a giggling shriek, and her peachy, freckled cheeks flushed pink with excitement. "There's no way she'll be able to do that!" she cried, and Rebecca shushed her.

"Which costume should we use?" Rebecca asked

in a low voice, and Tanya's ears perked up. The four girls were having a sleepover in Clio's aunt's costume and curio shop, Creature Features. The store was a crazy-quilt array of vintage wedding gowns, plastic vampire fangs, and everything in between. It also had the best collection of old books anywhere in their small town of Piper, Oregon, and it had been a favorite hangout spot for the girls since Clio's aunt, Kawanna, had opened it earlier that year.

Tanya glanced outside the storefront window. It was well past dinnertime, but early enough that people were still strolling the narrow sidewalks of Coffin Street on their way back from the restaurants on Main Street. Were her friends going to dare her to put on a costume and walk around the block? Tanya hoped not. In her opinion, there were two kinds of people: those who were costume people, and those who were not. Tanya was firmly in the *Not* category. She found costumes infinitely stressful, and every time she had to wear one, she secretly worried she'd show up and discover that she was the only one dressed up. She hated being the center of attention, and her Halloween costumes were always minimal unless the other girls convinced her to be part of a group ensemble.

Maggie pulled a bright yellow bird suit off the

rack. It was covered in fluffy feathers and had a hood with an orange beak. "What about this one?" she asked in a low voice.

Rebecca grinned and clapped her hands. "Perfect!" she whispered.

"I'll get the tights," Clio suggested, and Tanya could already feel her cheeks and ears going hot. *Tights?* This was going to be way more embarrassing than she thought.

Tanya stood up and ran her hand over her dark, pixie-cut hair. "All right, whatever you have planned, let's just get this over with."

"Not so fast," a voice said. Kawanna Carter appeared in the doorway that led to her cozy little apartment in the back of the shop. She wore a faded pair of gray Juilliard sweatpants with a soft navy-blue T-shirt, and her long dreadlocks were pulled back in a loose ponytail at the nape of her neck. She held an enormous metal bowl of buttery popcorn in her arms. "I just finished getting the snacks together, and I can't have all of you scampering off before you've even tasted them." She placed the bowl on the glass counter, elbowing aside a plastic skull to make room. "How about you girls run to the kitchen and grab the other things? Clio, there's hot cocoa on the stove. Can you pour it into mugs for all of us?"

The girls all jumped up to help and hurried into the dark hallway. Clio called to her aunt, "Why are all the lights off back here?"

"I'm conserving energy," Kawanna called back. "Didn't you hear that NPR story on polar bears this morning?"

Clio flipped the hallway light switch, but nothing happened. "Well, now the bulb isn't even working."

Tanya unhooked a key chain flashlight from her waistband and clicked it on. Clio turned around. "Where did that come from?"

"I always keep a little flashlight clipped to my waistband. You know that."

"Yeah, but you're in your *pajamas*," Clio answered.

"Which is exactly when you need a flashlight," Tanya said. "Don't you ever read under the covers past your bedtime?"

"Whoa," Clio said, her eyes widening. "I think I need a pajama flashlight now, too!"

Tanya led the way down the narrow hallway, the tiny pocket beam making a small circle of light on the floor in front of her. Their shadows slid along the walls, oozing and pooling into corners. "Ugh," Maggie said. "This is bringing up way too many creepy memories."

Tanya turned around and pointed the flashlight

up under her chin, giving her face a spooky glow. "Don't worry, Mags. A little darkness never hurt anybody." She continued down the hallway and aimed the light into the pitch-black kitchen.

The beam lit on a hideous, snarling face with bulging, yellow eyes. The skin, scarred with gashes, sagged loosely, giving the impression that the creature's whole head was slowly melting.

Three of the girls screamed and wheeled around. They ran back down the hallway, where a chuckling Kawanna stood waiting for them. Kawanna flipped the hall light back on, and her coppery cheeks split into a wide smile.

"I thought the hall light was broken," Clio said accusingly.

Kawanna's face was impish. "I just loosened the bulb a little bit so it wouldn't turn on for you."

Clio shook her head. "You are too much, Auntie!" Clio's aunt had a puckish sense of humor, and she loved playing pranks on the girls. "You scared us half to death!"

"Not all of you," Kawanna pointed out. She winked at Tanya, who was planted near the kitchen doorway with a satisfied smirk on her face. "What gave it away, Little Miss Scientist?" she asked Tanya.

"Well, you seemed way too eager to send us down

a dark hallway, and NPR didn't do any polar bear stories this morning. I knew you had to be up to something." Tanya turned off her flashlight and clipped it back to her waistband. "Although, to be honest, we should all be working harder to conserve energy. It helps cut down on greenhouse gas emissions, and it's one of the simplest ways we can fight climate change."

Maggie ran over to Tanya and gently pushed past her into the kitchen. "Sounds like a great conversation for another time." She flipped on the kitchen light switch. "Right now I want to see what Kawanna used to scare us. Plus, snacks!" Maggie tapped the stuffed rubber mask that Kawanna had hung from the ceiling fan with black thread and gave an approving nod. "Nice one," she said. Then she spied the plate of chocolate cupcakes on the counter. "Ooh, Rebecca, did you make those?"

Rebecca scooped up the plate with one hand and a stack of napkins with the other. "Yup. They have a molten salted caramel center."

"What? Those sound amazing!" Clio used an oven mitt to pour the pot of cocoa into five mugs, each with a different monster face. "Who wants the mummy?"

"I'll take it," Tanya said. "I love mummies." Clio

handed off the cocoa to Tanya and plunked a pile of marshmallows into a skull mug for Maggie.

"Ooh, marshmallows. You know me too well!" Maggie grabbed it along with a bowl of candy. "And, Tanya, you are one lovable weirdo. Seriously, who else in the world would say they love *mummies?*"

"*I* love mummies." Clio handed out the last of the cocoa.

"Yeah, but that's different," Maggie said. "Your parents are history professors, so you kind of have to."

"I don't think it really works that way." Rebecca took a sip from her werewolf mug. "My parents are both doctors, and I hate blood and guts and stuff."

Maggie followed Rebecca out of the kitchen. "Well, you're outnumbered. Tanya's dad's an engineer, and she's all about STEM. And my mom's a banker, and you know I love money."

With her free arm, Tanya scooped up a bowl of potato chips and joined the snack caravan back to the shop, shutting the light off with her elbow. The rubber mask spun lazily at the end of the thread, and Tanya smiled and shook her head. Kawanna sure knew how to play a good prank.

Back in the shop, the girls piled paper plates high with snacks while Kawanna thumbed through her

DVD collection of classic horror movies. "What are you girls in the mood for tonight?" she asked.

"Let's pick something spooky enough that it'll finally scare Tanya," Maggie suggested. "Whenever the rest of us are jumping out of our skin, she *takes notes* in her little lab book. Like we have a run-in with a ghost or a ghoul or something, and instead of freaking out like a normal person, she's all, '*Oh, let's get a closer look so we can study it.*'"

"Hey, I get scared, too, you know," Tanya said. "Like when we're *actually* in danger. But as for all the supernatural stuff, I guess I just don't get spooked that easily."

Rebecca broke open her cupcake, revealing the gooey caramel inside. "I wish I could say that. I still cover my eyes when we watch *Buffy the Vampire Slayer*."

"I know one thing Tanya's afraid of, which is why this is going to be the best dare ever," Clio said. She held up the bird costume and a pair of orange-and-pink striped tights. "So get ready to put this on and do the Chicken Dance for Maggie's YouTube channel!"

Tanya groaned and covered her face, but she laughed along with the others. Maggie's channel had only nineteen subscribers, and most of them were members of Maggie's own family. Tanya picked up the costume and trudged to the dressing room to change.

"So when do you start your new babysitting job?" Clio called through the curtain.

"Next week," Tanya called back. She wrestled with the striped tights, which were somehow both too snug and too loose at the same time. "It's for my neighbor, Mrs. Fogelman. My parents ran into her at the farmers market, and she mentioned she was looking for a sitter."

"Isn't she the old lady in the house with all the wild sculptures in the yard?" Rebecca asked. "She seems a little old to have kids."

"Her great-niece is coming for a visit." Tanya yanked on the bird costume and tried not to get whacked in the face by the fountain of tail feathers that sprung from the back. "She's seven, and her name is Kira. Her mom's in the hospital for a while, so she's staying up here with her great-aunt until her mom gets better."

"That's a bummer," Maggie said. "Where's she from?"

"Los Angeles." Tanya pulled the beaked hood over her head and shrugged. Not so bad. The bright yellow of the costume felt like a blinking neon sign that screamed *Look at me!*, but it wasn't the worst thing in the world. She sucked in her cheeks for a moment, trying to make her lips look like a beak. Nope. It just looked like a typical fish face.

Maggie wailed, "Los Angeles? That poor girl is going to be so bored when she sees this tiny town!"

"Oh, don't be so hard on Piper," Kawanna chided playfully. "LA was a fun place to live, but once I came to this town, I never looked back. I love it here!"

Tanya pulled open the curtain and marched out of the dressing room. She flapped her strapped-on wings. "Well? How do I look?"

"OMG, it's perfect!" Maggie shrieked.

Rebecca and Clio hooted. "Yes!" Clio hollered. "I am the dare master!"

Maggie dragged Tanya in front of a green sheet she had pinned up on one wall. "Now stand here in front of the green screen."

"I've got the music all cued up," Kawanna said.

Maggie aimed her phone's camera at Tanya. "And three . . . two . . . one . . . action!" The music started and Tanya flapped, clapped, and wriggled, her cheeks flaming scarlet. Rebecca and Clio collapsed in a giggling heap on the floor, and Kawanna made a potato chip duck beak and danced along behind the counter.

The light from the shop windows spilled golden pools onto the sidewalk outside. It was past closing time for the restaurants now, and a few stragglers scurried past, slowing down for a curious glance before quickening their steps, eager to get home and escape the cold winter air.

And from the rooftop across the street, a great horned owl spread its wings and took flight, heading in the direction of the dark forest beyond the town's borders.

CHAPTER 2

THE OLD WOMAN stood at the sink. Pink rivulets of water swirled against the white porcelain. Crimson bloomed on snowy linen. The doll's painted eyes blinked. The head turned, and the blank eyes sharpened, locking on her own.

Tanya woke up with a gasp, pulling herself out of the nightmare like a diver desperate for air. She still clutched her pillow in a death grip, and her pajama top was soaked through with cold sweat. Again. "It was just a bad dream. Just another meaningless bad dream," she whispered to herself. She unclenched her fists and cracked her knuckles, surprised at the ache in her fingers; she must have been clutching her pillow for hours. A cut on her finger throbbed angry and red, even though it was over a week old. It had

been fine before bed; she must have inflamed it in her sleep. A drop of blood oozed from one corner.

The sight of blood made her think of the dream again, and Tanya shuddered and switched on her bedside lamp. She looked around her cozy, familiar bedroom, smoothing the bright patchwork quilt her mom had made for her out of the family's old T-shirts. There was her ceiling, painted indigo like the evening sky, with pale green glow-in-the-dark stars arranged in constellations that stretched to every corner. The walls of her room were a bright spring green, broken up by science posters, cutouts from her parents' old *National Geographic* magazines, and the free calendar she had gotten for her donation to the World Wildlife Fund. January's picture featured a mother pangolin with a baby riding on her back. Tanya took a deep breath and let it out, just like her parents had taught her to do when she felt anxious. *See?* she thought. *These are my things. This is my room. I'm fine.*

Tanya climbed out of her twin bed, grimacing at the sweaty dent she had left in the mattress. She pulled off her clammy shirt and tossed it on top of the still-damp one she had changed out of after her last nightmare, just a few hours ago. She picked out another shirt from her closet and slipped it on. It was one of her brother's old tees, with a bicycle on the front and a hole near the hem. The fabric was soft and cool, and she immediately felt a little better.

The dreams had left Tanya rattled. She had heard her friends talk about the nightmares they got sometimes, especially after they all started tangling with the supernatural beings that seemed to crop up all over their small town. But Tanya had never really had many bad dreams until recently.

She opened the notebook she kept beside her bed and used one hand to search absently for the mechanical pencil she always had next to it. She heard the pencil roll behind the headboard, so she grabbed another one from the cup near the microscope on top of her desk. A sliver of cloudy mirror was clamped to the microscope's stage, and Tanya scowled at it and shook her injured finger. She could still see a tiny bit of rust-colored blood from where she had cut herself on the sharp edge. She wrote down what she could remember of the dream, noting the date and time: *Same dream again. Old woman spoon-feeding a doll. I think it's blood? Painted eyes, but doll blinks. Moves. It can see me.*

She leafed back through the other entries in the notebook. Many of them were about the paranormal encounters she had experienced with her friends, and the notes included diagrams, charts, and tables she had drawn and filled out in her tiny, cramped handwriting. Some were organized as formal lab reports, but others were just notes, observations, and impressions. Tanya wasn't sure why she had decided to include the dreams in the notebook; they didn't seem particularly scientific, and they weren't supernatural, either. They were just weird. And scary.

When Maggie and Rebecca mentioned their nightmares, they always seemed related to things that had already happened: a rotting arm pulling them into a hole; a feast turning to worms in their hands. In every one of their nightmares, the Night Queen was present, her deep blue face twisted into a cruel smile, spider-leg hair sprouting from her crown like a mane. Clio was quieter, but when she did talk about her bad dreams, they were always about the Night Queen, too. Tanya recorded those into the notebook because they were linked to all of the other supernatural events in town. But Tanya's dreams didn't seem to be related to anything at all.

She looked at the clock on her nightstand. By now it was almost morning, so there was no point in going back to sleep. She might as well get some work done in the meantime. She switched on her microscope and flipped to a clean page in her notebook before collecting her chemistry set from the bookshelf.

When she moved it aside, she found two unblinking eyes staring back at her. She jumped, stifling a scream and barely avoiding dropping the box in her hands. It was a doll. Her grandparents in Oaxaca, Mexico, used to send her one each birthday when she was little, but it had been years since she had played with them, and she had forgotten she still had them. Tanya carried the chemistry set back to her desk, making a mental note to video chat with her grandparents later in the week. They had talked a lot over the holidays, but things had gotten busy now that the winter break was over and school had started again.

Tanya repositioned the mirror shard on the microscope's stage, careful not to cut her hand again. She looked through the eyepiece and adjusted the focus. The flecks in the silvery glass were crisp, their outlines sharp. Tanya felt the familiar thrill she always got when working on a scientific problem, and she was especially interested in this one. The shard was part of an antique mirror the Night Queen had used to communicate with her minions in Piper; Tanya thought of it as a kind of supernatural version of a video chat. She wondered if there might be something special about the mirror's chemical composition that would reveal how the queen was able to use it.

She had just used a dropper to place a tiny amount

of hydrochloric acid on the sliver of glass when the hairs on the back of her neck prickled. Someone was watching her. Tanya was in no mood to deal with interruptions from her older brother. She kept her eye trained on the bubbling glass of her experiment. "Knock it off, Bryce. I'm working." There was no answer. Tanya turned around. The room was empty.

Tanya tried to refocus on the microscope, but she couldn't shake the feeling of being watched. She turned around again. Where was it coming from?

That's when she noticed the doll on her shelf again. The eyes were dark brown, and it looked nothing like the doll in her dream. But still, it was unsettling to feel those lifeless eyes staring at her like that. Creepy. *That's silly.* Tanya shook her head. *It's just a doll.* She turned back to her experiment, but now she had missed the full reaction. She would have to start over. She ran her hands over her face and sighed. She was tired.

As Tanya started to prep the new sample, a thought popped into her mind, unbidden. *What if right now, behind me, that doll just blinked and I couldn't see it?* Tanya almost dropped the bottle in her hand. *Stop it*, Tanya told herself. *It didn't. It can't.* "It can't," she repeated out loud to reassure herself. "Dreams aren't real. Dolls don't move." She bent over the microscope again, the nape of her neck suddenly feeling bare and exposed. *How do you know dolls don't move?* her treacherous brain asked her, suddenly. *How do you know that doll isn't sneaking up on you right this second?* Tanya's chest tightened, and she whirled around. The doll sat unmoving on her shelf, just as the rational part of her brain knew it would be.

But she didn't want to turn around again. She didn't like the feeling of standing with her back to the doll. Tanya stood frozen in place. "This is ridiculous," she said, her voice sounding loud in her ears. "I'm not in danger. There's literally no reason to be scared." Another thought snuck into her brain. *Yeah, but you're scared anyway.* She tried to push the thought away, but she knew that it was true.

She stood still for another minute, and then she walked over to her closet and yanked open the door. She dragged out a green plastic bin and dumped its contents on the floor. Swiftly, and without thinking, she grabbed the doll and tossed it in the bin. With shaking hands, she quickly rummaged through the rest of her shelves until all her other dolls were gone. She jammed them down and snapped on the lid tightly. Then she got a roll of duct tape from her desk drawer and wrapped it several times around before she was satisfied. She used a marker to write FOR

CHARITY on a piece of scrap paper and taped the paper to the lid.

Careful not to wake anyone, she carried the bin downstairs and tucked it next to the door to the garage. *Problem solved*, she thought. *Now I can get back to work.* She went back upstairs and sat at her desk, forcing herself to concentrate on her notes. Again she set up the sample on the microscope, and again she prepared the eyedropper of acid. But all the while, she couldn't help thinking about the bin downstairs and the pile of dolls lying quietly inside it like corpses in a coffin.

CHAPTER 3

MRS. FOGELMAN WAS already standing in the front doorway by the time Tanya had closed the gate behind her and started up the walk to the porch of the red clapboard house. Tanya checked her watch. She was ten minutes early. How long had the woman been waiting for her? Tanya waved and smiled, expecting to see Kira beside her great-aunt, but the little girl was nowhere to be seen.

"Hi, Mrs. Fogelman," Tanya said. "I'm excited to meet Kira. Is she inside?"

"Oh, who knows?" Mrs. Fogelman said. "I needed a break. Honestly, she's been here two days and all she's done is complain about everything." She waved one hand, and the stack of Bakelite bracelets on her wrist rattled. "You'd think the world would end without Wi-Fi."

Tanya didn't know Mrs. Fogelman well, but it seemed like a strange way to talk about a great-niece, especially one who had a sick mother back home. Tanya studied the woman in front of her. Her dark hair was streaked with gray and framed her face in wild tendrils that fell to her shoulders. She had olive skin and strong cheekbones with heavy eyebrows above large, hazel eyes. Draped over her sturdy frame was a long, embroidered caftan in rich jewel tones that matched her dark berry lipstick. Tanya had heard the neighbors describe Mrs. Fogelman as "eccentric," but Tanya's parents just said that artists couldn't be expected to act like everyone else.

"Let me introduce you to Kira, and then I'll leave you to it. I'll be working in my studio behind the house. I'm in the midst of a very important sculpture, and I absolutely *must* get back to it!" Tanya followed the woman down the hall, catching glimpses of brightly painted rooms that were filled with bookshelves, interesting collections, and art of all kinds. It seemed like the kind of house Kawanna would like, and it made Tanya feel a little warmer toward Mrs. Fogelman than she had before.

In the sunroom at the back of the house, Tanya found a pinched-face girl with sallow skin and wavy blond hair. Her pale blue eyes stared down at the hand-held screen in front of her. "Kira," Mrs. Fogelman said a little too loudly, "your playmate, Tanya, is here. Wouldn't you like to say hello?"

Kira's eyes flicked up from the screen. "Oh, hi," she said. She quickly took in Tanya's ratty jeans, Doctor Who scarf, and old army jacket before she went back to her screen. "Nice to meet you," she added faintly, her voice already blurry with disinterest.

"Nice to meet you, too," Tanya answered, suddenly self-conscious about the forced cheer she could hear in her voice. "So, what would you like to do together today?" Kira didn't answer.

Mrs. Fogelman sighed. "See what I'm up against?" she murmured under her breath. Tanya felt a surge of sympathy for the artist. Most seven-year-olds that Tanya knew were sunny kids, curious about the world and eager to please, but trying to talk to this girl felt like talking to an empty room. Tanya tucked her bag near the couch, thinking of all the fun games and activities she had planned and carefully packed into it. It seemed doubtful the bag would even get opened today.

Mrs. Fogelman looked between the two girls.

"Well," she said finally, with a brisk clap of her hands. "I'll leave you two to it, then!" She pointed through the windows to a small detached garage behind the house. "I'll be out in my studio if you need me, but please don't disturb me unless you absolutely must." She ran her hands through her wild hair. "I'm at a critical stage in my work, and when the art speaks to me like this, I am fully in its thrall. I'm sure you understand!"

Tanya didn't, but she nodded and smiled. "You bet."

"Kira, why don't you take Tanya upstairs and show her the collection room? I'm sure you girls would love to play up there together!" Without waiting for an answer, she exited in a swirl of jewel tones and clattering bangles, leaving a fog of sandalwood perfume in her wake.

"Do you want to show me the collection room?" Tanya asked. "It sounds like it could be fun to check it out."

Tanya stood in front of the couch for a moment waiting for a cue from Kira, but the little girl continued to ignore her. Usually Tanya liked to let the kids have a say in how they spent their time together, but this was clearly going to be different. She wished Mrs. Fogelman had referred to her as a babysitter instead of a playmate. How was she supposed to take charge of the situation if Kira thought she was just here to be a friend? Not that it seemed likely that Kira would be any more willing to listen to her either way.

"Okay, Kira," Tanya said finally. "Time to put your device away." When the little girl didn't look up, Tanya crouched down so she was at eye level. "Kira," she said firmly. "No more screens while I'm here."

Kira finally looked up. "Why not? My parents let me have as much screen time as I want." She went back to her game. "Besides, there's nothing else to do here."

Tanya sighed inwardly. Kira seemed determined to turn their first interaction into a battle of wills. Tanya had babysat for some tough kids before, but they didn't usually start testing her right away like this. She decided to try a different tactic. "Okay, then. I'll be in the kitchen, I guess, working on my experiment." She picked up her bag and left the sunroom, making sure not to look back.

There was a pause, then Kira took the bait. "What experiment?" she called after her.

"It's just science stuff. Nothing you'd be interested in." Tanya put an eyedropper and a bag of pennies on the counter next to a clipboard and a pencil.

She smiled to herself when she heard bare feet padding into the kitchen.

"What's the clipboard for?" Kira asked. Tanya mentally gave herself a high five. No kid could ever resist a clipboard.

"As a scientist, I have to write down everything that happens in my experiment, so I organize it all here on this chart." Tanya showed Kira the chart she had created and printed out with each column neatly labeled. She found a small bowl and filled it with water. "Anyway, you can get back to your game now. I'll try to keep it down so I don't bother you." She slowly filled the eyedropper with water.

Kira plunked her device onto the counter, her eyes watching Tanya's every move. "Can I help?"

Tanya acted surprised. "Oh! Sure, I guess so. But we should probably put your device away so it doesn't get wet. My experiments get messy sometimes. Why don't you put it back in your room while I get started?" She laid two pennies out on the counter.

Kira was already running toward the stairs. "Wait! Don't start without me!" she cried over her shoulder, and Tanya grinned.

"Just another reason why science is so awesome," she said, pulling the second eyedropper out of her bag.

Kira's cheeks were flushed when she got back to the kitchen. "Did I miss anything?" she asked breathlessly.

"No, I waited for you," Tanya answered. "I wanted to give you a chance to form a hypothesis before we start. A hypothesis is a sort of prediction. In this case, we're trying to predict how many drops of water will fit on top of a penny. What do you think?"

Kira thought for a moment. "One," she said finally. "A penny's not very big."

"I like how you thought about the size of the penny when you made your prediction," Tanya said. "Scientists try to look at all the data before they make a hypothesis, just like you did." The corners of Kira's mouth turned up in a shy smile.

Tanya slid a penny in front of her and handed her an eyedropper. "Okay, are you ready to test it out? Let's count each drop out loud."

Kira squirted out one drop. "One," they said together. "Two. Three . . ." Kira's eyes grew wide as the number continued to climb, and the bead of liquid on top of the penny ballooned larger and larger. The surface tension of the water finally broke and spilled across the counter. Tanya wiped it up with a rag and showed Kira where on the chart to record the number of drops.

"I want to see if we can fit more!" Kira said. "Can we try it again?"

· · · · ·

Kira was soon chattering away, and the rest of the afternoon passed easily. Tanya learned that Kira had a best friend named Arthur back in LA, that her favorite food was tacos, and that she missed her parents back home.

"My mom has cancer," Kira said. "My parents said the doctors think the surgery will get rid of it, but that it's going to take time for her to heal."

"Are you worried about her?" Tanya asked. She remembered when Rebecca's grandmother got sick a few years ago and how hard it was for the family to see their lively matriarch grow frail and quiet.

"I'm mostly mad," Kira answered. "They made me come up here to stay with Auntie Dot until Mom feels better. I wanted to stay home and help, but they wouldn't let me. They act like I'm a baby or something!"

Tanya put away the eye droppers and wiped up the last of the water from the counter. "I get it; I would want to help, too. But I bet your parents don't mean to treat you like a baby; sometimes people just need a quiet place to get better." She held up the two pennies.

"One for you, and one for me. A souvenir of our day together."

Kira took the shinier one and put it in her pocket. "What should we do now?"

"Do you want to give me a tour of the house? I've never been here before, and your great-aunt said something about a room where she keeps all of her collections."

Kira waved her hand. "Auntie Dot has a lot of collections; there's no way she could keep them all in one room. See? Look at this." She pointed at a shelf that wound above the cabinets near the kitchen ceiling. "That's her teapot collection." Teapots of every shape and color marched along the shelves in perfect precision. Tanya spied a purple one shaped like a dragon. Another looked like an elephant with the spout as its trunk. "And wait 'til you see the dining room. She calls it her 'green room.'"

Tanya followed her into a cozy dining room with gleaming wood floors and bottle-green silk wallpaper. A gilded china cabinet dominated one wall, and it was crammed with glasses and dishes in every shade of green. A green glass chandelier hung from the gold-painted ceiling over the mirrored gold dining table and green velvet chairs. "Whoa," Tanya said.

"Auntie Dot says green's her favorite color," Kira said.

"Obviously," Tanya said. "I mean, it's my favorite color, too, but this is, like, green on steroids."

Kira shrugged. "She says it grows on you."

"I guess," Tanya said skeptically. "Is every room like this?"

"Kind of," Kira answered. As she led Tanya through the rest of the first floor, Tanya could see what the neighbors meant when they called Mrs. Fogelman eccentric. It wasn't that there was anything wrong with the house; it was just decorated unlike any other home Tanya had ever seen. The stairwell ceiling was painted bright blue with fluffy white clouds, and the walls were lined with mirrors, reflecting infinite Tanyas back at one another as they climbed up to the second floor.

Kira showed Tanya the guest room where she was staying. It reminded Tanya of the Enchanted Tiki Room at Disneyland. The walls were papered with some kind of woven bamboo, and the canopy of the four-poster bed was grass thatch. Glass globe lights hung from the ceiling in rope nets, and the bedside table had a hula-girl lamp. Although it didn't exactly look like a kid's bedroom, it seemed like it could be a fun place to stay for a while. There were a few stuffed animals perched on the tropical-print bedspread, which Tanya assumed Kira had brought with her. "This is a neat room."

Kira shrugged. "It's okay, I guess. My bedroom at home is pink and gold, and my comforter has a puppy on it."

"That sounds cool," Tanya said. "Do you like dogs?"

"I love them!" Kira gushed. She continued down the hall. "My mom and dad promised we're going to get a rescue dog after my mom gets better. I already picked out a name for him and everything! I want to call him Max."

"Cool," Tanya answered. She followed Kira to the closed door at the end of the hall. "What's in here?"

"This is the collection room Auntie Dot was talking about." Kira turned the knob and opened the door. When Tanya saw what was inside, the smile fell away from her face.

The room was filled with hundreds of dolls.

Rows and rows of them were crammed onto the shelves that lined the cream-colored walls, and still more were nestled among the lacy pillows on the brass daybed. Tucked next to the bed was a white wicker bassinet with a realistic-looking baby doll swaddled inside. In the corner stood a child-sized table and chairs where a quartet of larger dolls were seated for a tea party, complete with miniature china cups. A thousand unblinking eyes seemed to stare back at Tanya wherever she looked, and she found herself growing dizzy. She took a deep breath and gripped the edge of the daybed for support. "What . . . uh . . ." Tanya steeled herself and tried to act natural. "What is this?"

"It's Auntie Dot's doll collection. She has dolls from all over the world, and some of them are really old. She's been collecting them since she was a little girl. Do you want to see any of them?"

Tanya's smile was wan, and her knuckles were white where her fingers wrapped around the daybed's rail. "That's okay. Unless you want to show them to me. I'm not really a doll person."

"Me neither," Kira answered. "I like stuffed animals."

"Same," said Tanya, relieved. She edged toward the hallway. "Do you want to go back downstairs?"

"Sure," Kira said. "Can you believe my Auntie Dot wanted me to sleep in here?"

"She *did*?" Tanya asked, horrified. There was no way she would ever sleep in that room, not for all the money in the world.

"Uh-huh," Kira said. "She was all excited to show it to me when I first got here. She said it was 'perfect for a little girl.' I said, 'Maybe for a girl a hundred years ago, but I don't know any girl who would want to stay in a bedroom like that.' She got kind of angry after that and went out to her studio for a long time."

"Yeah, I think there was probably a nicer way you could have told her that," Tanya said.

"Why?" Kira asked. "I didn't even want to come stay here in the first place." Her eyebrows knitted together. "I'm bored. Didn't you bring anything else to do?"

"Oh! Uh, yeah, sure." Tanya was thrown by the sudden change in mood. "Let's go back downstairs." She took one last nervous look inside and caught the tiniest movement. Her senses sharpened, and she peered more closely at the sea of eyes, but all was still. Tanya shuddered and shut the door firmly behind her, cursing her overactive imagination. She ignored the cold sweat that had broken out on her forehead, and she forced enthusiasm into her voice. "I have a great idea for a game!" But the prickle at the back of her neck remained.

Tanya could swear one of the dolls had winked at her.

CHAPTER 4

TANYA LEANED AGAINST her locker and took a final look at her algebra homework before putting it away. She had finished it early in class, and even though she already knew it was perfect she couldn't help checking it again. Something about seeing all of those problems neatly completed on the page made her heart sing a little, and she flipped it over to check the back. Oops. She had used the corner of the graph paper to sketch out a diagram for a new invention idea she had. She hoped Mr. Benjamin wouldn't mind.

"Ugh, I wish I was in the same math class as you," Maggie said, peering over Tanya's shoulder. "But no, you have to be in algebra with all the other geeks and leave me behind in Math Achievers." Maggie pushed up the sleeves of her pink sweatshirt and twisted around to make sure the silver angel wings printed on the back showed around the straps of her glittery backpack. "I'm still not sure how to divide mixed numbers or why I'd even want to, and there are people in there in even worse shape than me. Calling us 'math achievers' is just embarrassing for everyone involved."

"Sorry, Mags," Tanya answered. "I will never give up my geekiness."

Maggie slammed her locker shut with a smile. "I know, you miserable traitor." Tanya laughed, and Maggie gave her a squeeze. "But I love you anyway."

Rebecca checked her braid crown in her locker mirror and tightened the backings on her hoop earrings. "I can help you with math if you need it. I've gotten As on all my pre-algebra tests so far."

"No thanks," Maggie answered. "Every time you try to help me you just end up complaining that my work is too messy to read."

"That's because it is." Rebecca buckled her caramel leather backpack and slung it onto her shoulders. "But I guess not everyone can be perfect like meee," she sang.

Clio laughed. "Perfect is one way to put it, I guess." She fluffed her twist-outs and slipped on a bright yellow headband. "Some of us might call it . . . obsessive."

Rebecca raised her eyebrows in mock offense.

"What? Just because I color-code my assignments? I prefer to think of myself as detail oriented."

The girls started walking down the hall toward the cafeteria. "Are we meeting Ethan for lunch?" Maggie asked, looking at Clio.

"Why are you asking me?" Clio said. "We're *all* friends with Ethan, you know."

"Yeah, I know," Maggie said. "So, are we?" she asked her again.

Clio bit her lip and tried not to smile. "He said he'd see us there."

"He did, huh?" Maggie nudged Clio with her elbow. "When did he say that? You don't have any classes together."

Clio wouldn't look at Maggie. "He texted me."

Maggie grinned and nudged Clio again. "He texted you, huh?"

"Oh, come on! You text me all the time!"

Maggie waggled her eyebrows. "Yeah, but *I'm* not Ethan!"

When the girls got to the cafeteria, Ethan Underwood was sitting at their usual table bent over a book, his blue-streaked bangs hanging down over his eyes. He jumped up and waved when he saw the girls walking over. "What's up? Oh, hey, Clio. I like your shirt."

Clio's eyelashes lowered shyly, and she touched

the neck of her embroidered peasant blouse. "Oh, thanks." She sat next to Ethan in the chair he had pulled out for her. Ethan's pale cheeks were flushed scarlet when he took his seat again, and he bent his head back over the book, hiding behind his bangs.

Tanya took pity on him. "What are you reading?"

Ethan looked around before answering to make sure nobody would overhear, a sure sign that it must be something supernatural. The girls leaned in closer.

Ethan's voice was soft. "I found it in Great-Grandma Moina's collection. It's a book about object possession." Ethan's great-great-grandmother had worked as a psychic medium back in the 1920s, and Ethan had inherited both her records and her supernatural abilities. Well, mostly. He was still figuring it out.

"Object possession?" Rebecca asked. "Is it a book about supernatural property law or something?" She laughed and looked around the table. "Get it, guys? Object possession? Property law?" The others just stared at her. She shrugged. "Whatever. I thought it was a good joke," she mumbled.

"It wasn't," Maggie said. "But that's okay; you just rock on with your nerdy self."

"Object possession is when ordinary stuff takes on an entity of some kind and it basically becomes haunted," Ethan explained.

"Oh, like when my parents took me on a ghost tour at this castle in Rhode Island," Maggie said. "It was full of ghost stories. There was this suit of armor with the helmet bashed in, and the tour guide said that sometimes it would shriek at night." Maggie held up her arm and pointed to the gooseflesh that had sprouted on it. "Still gives me chills."

"Oh, that is so awful," Rebecca said. "Imagine being alone in a castle, and all of a sudden you hear random screaming." She shuddered. "It's like an endless jump-scare!"

"I don't know, Becks," Maggie said. "We've dealt with some really freaky stuff when we've babysat. Is a screaming suit of armor really any worse?"

"Yes!" Rebecca answered. "It's the whole startle factor. You know I hate being startled!"

Maggie unwrapped the foil from her leftover pizza. "Oh, okay, cool. So we're still good to go as long as the Night Queen doesn't pop out unexpectedly and yell, 'Boo!'"

"Pretty much." Rebecca took a bite of her turkey sandwich.

Tanya peeked over Ethan's shoulder. "So what does the book say? Are there certain elements or chemicals that the objects have in common?" she asked, thinking of the mirror pieces she was studying at home.

"Not really," Ethan said. "It could be anything: boxes, cabinets, books, furniture . . . pretty much whatever."

"What about portals and stuff? Does it talk about that?" Tanya asked.

Ethan pushed the book over to Tanya. "I don't think so. It's more a collection of spooky stories about possessed objects than anything else, but you can borrow it if you want. Maybe you can find something in here that I'm missing."

"Thanks," Tanya said. She tucked the book in her backpack and spooned a bite of vegetarian chili from the thermos her dad had packed her.

Clio reached across and tapped Tanya on the arm. "You still haven't said much about your new baby-sitting gig. How was it?"

Tanya opened a bag of tortilla chips and dipped one into the chili. "It was okay. Kira's a little bit hot-and-cold, and she and Mrs. Fogelman don't seem very close. It's not terrible, but it's definitely not the easiest babysitting job I've ever had. I feel a little sorry for both of them."

"That sounds kind of tricky," Rebecca said. She put her empty sandwich container back in her lunch bag and picked up a slice of cucumber. "But at least nothing supernatural happened, right?"

"Right." Tanya thought back to the roomful of dolls. Sure, they scared her, but lots of people thought dolls were weird and unsettling. It wasn't like anything had actually happened. *Except for that doll that winked at you.* The thought tried to bubble its way to the surface, but she pushed it back down. *Nothing winked at me. I just let my imagination get the best of me.* "Everything was totally normal," she said firmly. She took a long sip from her water bottle.

"Well, that's a relief," Maggie said. "Because if any other spooky things happen in this town, we are seriously all going to have to move away to someplace safe and boring, like Iowa. And I do *not* want to live in Iowa!"

"Hey, don't harsh on Iowa," Tanya said. "My cousin Julie lives there!"

"Uh-huh. And how does Julie like living in Iowa?" Maggie challenged.

"I don't know," Tanya admitted. "They're moving to Chicago."

Maggie tossed her pizza crust triumphantly down on the table. "I rest my case!"

"Nobody's moving to Iowa," Clio said. She checked her phone and stood up. "But I do have to move it if I want to get to history on time."

Tanya stood up. "Yeah, I should head out, too.

Spanish is all the way on the other side of the building." She tapped Ethan on the shoulder. "Thanks for the book. I'll give it back to you as soon as I can."

"No worries, keep it as long as you want," Ethan replied.

Tanya waved goodbye to her friends and slipped Ethan's book out of her backpack to read on the way to class. It was a leather-bound book with a green cover, and the title was written in plain block letters: *Object Possession*. She riffled through the pages, pausing when she came to the etched illustrations. One showed a couple quailing at a tendril of vapor seeping from a wine cabinet, and Tanya rolled her eyes. She and her friends had literally fought off zombies, and the adults in this book were afraid of a little wisp of smoke?

Object possession was an interesting idea, though. It wasn't exactly possession, but the girls *had* found certain places and things the Night Queen was able to control. Ethan's book seemed like more stories than science, but if it could give Tanya a clue to what they had in common, it might be a powerful tool to defeat the Night Queen once and for all.

CHAPTER 5

WHEN TANYA KNOCKED on Mrs. Fogelman's door a few days later, it was Kira who answered it. "Auntie Dot said you were coming today." She tried to peek into the tote bag Tanya was carrying. "Did you bring any experiments?"

"I did," Tanya said. "It might get a little messy, so you have to promise to help clean up." She followed Kira into the kitchen and began unpacking the bag on the counter.

Kira's eyes widened when Tanya pulled out a head of red cabbage. "What's that for?"

"You'll see," Tanya answered. She lined up a small bottle of white vinegar next to a lemon and a box of baking soda. Finally, she took out a container of chewable antacid tablets. "Now we just need a knife and a cutting board so I can chop up this cabbage."

Mrs. Fogelman swept into the room. Her striking, silver-streaked hair was pulled up in a messy bun around her head, and she wore a vivid orange-and-green caftan with a pair of beaded leather sandals. Tanya wasn't much for fashion, but even she thought it was strange that anyone would wear sandals in the dead of winter. "I see Kira's already gotten you settled in. She did *so* enjoy your time together on Saturday. It looks like you have something equally enticing planned for today."

"I hope so," Tanya said. "As long as you don't mind a little cutting and cooking. We'll be careful, and we'll clean everything up afterward." Tanya took a bright blue pot off the stove top and filled it with water.

"It's fine with me. Just make sure nobody loses a finger. Her parents will be furious if I don't send her home in one piece!" Mrs. Fogelman gave a husky laugh and tossed a voluminous hand-knitted shawl over her shoulders, her bangles clattering merrily down her wrist. "I'm off to my studio." Her eyes blazed. "The work awaits!" A cloud of sandalwood scent followed her out the door.

Tanya searched through the drawers until she found a knife and a cutting board. "Your auntie Dot sure does love making art," she said. "Is she always this busy when you visit her?"

Kira shook her head. "She used to like to play with me a lot more, and so did Uncle Eli." She reached for the lemon and rolled it along the counter's edge.

"Uncle Eli?" Tanya asked. She thought Mrs. Fogelman's husband had died a long time ago, before Tanya was even born.

"He wasn't really my uncle. He was Auntie Dot's boyfriend. He lived in Seattle, but they liked to visit each other a lot. He was an artist, too. Last summer when I came to Oregon, Auntie Dot and Uncle Eli took me by the river and we all built fairy houses and painted pictures."

Tanya put the cabbage on the cutting board and carefully cut it into slices. "That sounds like a great day. Is he going to see you while you're here this time?"

Kira frowned and picked at the white sticker on the lemon rind. "He died last month."

Tanya stopped cutting. "Last month? Oh, I'm so sorry, Kira. That's awful! Your great-aunt must be heartbroken."

Kira peeled off the sticker and stuck it to the leg of her fuchsia leggings. "Yeah. Uncle Eli was really fun. Auntie Dot doesn't like to talk about him, but I think she misses him a lot, and that's how come she's always in her studio. They were making a sculpture together before he died."

Tanya chopped the cabbage until the leaves were in tiny pieces. No wonder Mrs. Fogelman seemed so distracted. Other than Rebecca's grandmother, Tanya had never had someone close to her pass away. She remembered crying when Rebecca's Nai Nai died, and for weeks afterward the Chin family had seemed to be in a sort of sad cocoon. "Well," she finally said as she washed the knife and put it away, "I'm sure it's not the same without your uncle Eli, but I bet your auntie Dot is happy to have you here. I know she loves you a lot."

Kira didn't say anything, but her face darkened. "I don't care. I just want to be back home in my own room with my own mom and dad. It's ugly and boring here, and everything is cold and wet. Auntie Dot never takes me to do anything fun." She poked at the pile of cabbage on the cutting board. "What are we even doing with this gross cabbage anyway?"

"Why don't you help me put it in this pot of water and we'll find out?" Tanya scooped a pile of cabbage into the pot of water on the stove. "See? Like this."

Kira scowled. "*You* do it. I don't feel like it!"

Tanya tried not to react to Kira's change in mood. "That's fine," she said, keeping her voice calm and light. She poured the rest of the cabbage into the pot of water and set it to boil. "It'll be ready in about ten minutes. Do you want to help me set up the rest of the experiment while we wait?"

"No," Kira said flatly. "I'm going upstairs to play."

"Oh, okay," Tanya said. "We can do that instead."

"No," Kira repeated. "I don't want you to come with me. I want to play by myself."

Tanya wasn't sure what to do. Kira was her responsibility, and Tanya was here to keep the little girl company. But Kira was clearly going through a lot, and maybe she needed some time alone. "How about if I finish setting up the experiment, and then I'll come get you when it's ready. Sound good?"

"Sure, I guess," Kira said, already leaving the room. "I don't really care." Tanya heard her footsteps shuffling up the stairs. She put soap on a scrub brush and raked it across the wooden cutting board. She had put a lot of time into planning a fun day for Kira, and she had even spent her own money on some of the supplies. It felt silly to set everything up if Kira wasn't even interested. Tanya put the cutting board in the drying rack. *Even if she doesn't like it, I still think it's a cool project.* Kira's moods seemed to shift so quickly. Maybe the little girl would come around again, just like she had the last time Tanya was here.

Tanya found some small juice glasses and poured a bit of lemon juice into one and white vinegar into another. She mixed baking soda and water in a third glass and left a few empty on the counter. When the timer went off, she carefully separated the cabbage from the water, which was now a deep purple color. She poured the purple water into a bowl and left it on the counter to cool. It was time to check on Kira.

Tanya walked up the steps slowly, planning out what she would do if Kira refused to come downstairs. What were you supposed to do if the kid you were hired to babysit wouldn't let you babysit them? There was nothing wrong with Kira playing alone upstairs, but it wasn't really the reason Mrs. Fogelman had brought Tanya over.

When she got to the top of the stairs, Tanya headed straight for Kira's room, expecting to see the little girl with her nose buried in her device, playing a game or watching something she had downloaded back in California. But Kira's room was empty, and her screen was thrown carelessly on a rattan chair in the corner of the room.

Tanya picked it up. The battery was almost dead. "Kira?" Tanya called. "Do you want to charge your device before you come downstairs?" There was no answer. Tanya tapped on the closed door of the en suite bathroom. "Kira?" she called again. She didn't hear a reply, so Tanya opened the door a few inches. "Are you in there?" The bathroom was dark. She flipped on the light. The room was empty. Where could she be?

Tanya went back into the hallway. All the doors along it were closed. Could she have gone into her great-aunt's bedroom? Mrs. Fogelman had never explicitly said that the girls weren't allowed in her room, but Tanya wouldn't feel comfortable letting Kira play in there without asking her great-aunt first. Tanya opened the door. "Kira?" Tanya took in a carved rosewood bed and magenta walls covered in bold, abstract paintings before closing the door again and moving on.

Finally, after checking a small office and another bathroom, Tanya's steps slowed and she felt her chest tighten as she came to the last door. The doll room. She paused before touching the knob. Kira obviously wouldn't be in there; she said she didn't like dolls. No need to open the door and see all those glassy eyes staring back at her. *Just turn around*, she told herself. *Turn around and walk back downstairs. She'll come out when she's ready.*

Tanya gritted her teeth and forced herself to turn the knob. She wasn't going to let a ridiculous, irrational fear get in the way of doing her job. *If you're so brave, then why aren't you going inside?* she asked herself. "Good point," she said out loud, and pushed it open.

Day was waning outside, and the room was mostly

in shadow. Tanya flicked on the light and almost jumped out of her skin when she saw movement at the little table in the corner. She relaxed. It was only Kira.

"Why are you bothering me?" Kira's voice was sullen. "I'm *busy*."

"I can see that. What are you doing?" Tanya asked.

"Playing," Kira said. She turned her back to Tanya and picked up a small hairbrush from the table next to her.

"Oh." Tanya blinked. "I thought you didn't like dolls."

"Auntie Dot gave one to me. She says she's special."

"Wow. That's nice of her. Do you want to bring your new doll downstairs with you? Maybe she can help us with our experiment." Tanya hoped the girl would refuse. She was already unsettled by Kira's mercurial moods. Having some creepy doll hanging around would just put Tanya even more on edge.

"That's okay," Kira said. She put the hairbrush down. "I'm finished playing with her today."

"Good," Tanya answered, her voice sagging with relief. She shifted nervously. "I mean, I'm glad you had fun." She put her hands in her pockets. "So what did you play?"

"I held her and brushed her hair and fed her," Kira said proudly.

"That's great," Tanya said faintly.

"She was Auntie Dot's doll when she was a little girl, and before that she belonged to Auntie Dot's auntie, and before that she belonged to that auntie's auntie."

"Neat," Tanya said. Kira still wasn't turning around, and Tanya felt dizzy when she took in all the cold, waxy faces around her. Her legs felt weak, and she worked hard to focus just on the back of the little girl's head. "What's your doll's name?"

"Mary Rose," Kira said, and Tanya thought her legs would buckle under her. She gripped the door-jamb tightly. It had to be a coincidence. It had to be.

"Cool. So, uh, you ready to go downstairs, then?" Tanya backed away from the doorway so that she was all the way into the hall. The world around her seemed to contract to a tiny pinpoint, and she could hear the pounding of her heart.

"Your voice sounds weird. Are you okay?" Kira asked. She stood up and turned around, cradling the doll lovingly in her arms.

"I'm totally fine," Tanya answered, struggling to control the tremble in her voice. "I'm just excited to get back downstairs to our experiment." But it was fear and not excitement that gripped her.

The doll that Kira held was the same doll from Tanya's dream.

CHAPTER
6

KIRA LAID THE doll on the brass daybed and tucked a small quilted blanket around it. She kissed its forehead. "Good night, Mary Rose," Kira whispered. Tanya grimaced when she realized she was holding her breath; some part of her had actually expected Mary Rose to whisper back. Kira squirmed past, and Tanya closed the door firmly behind them. "Are you sick?" Kira asked. "You look like my mom does right before she throws up."

Tanya gave a wan smile. "It's nothing. I think I'm just a little tired." She pushed Mary Rose from her mind. It was a weird coincidence that she looked just like the doll in Tanya's dream, but a coincidence was all it was. Wasn't it? *Let it go. Bad dreams don't come to life*, Tanya told herself. *That's not how the world works. This isn't one of Maggie's movies.*

The sense of dread that had gripped her seemed to fade more and more as they got farther and farther from the doll room. *See?* Tanya thought. *You're fine. You were panicking over nothing.* Kira's mood had lightened, too, and she was already asking questions about the experiment on the way down the stairs. She slipped her hand in Tanya's, and Tanya felt a warm little glow in her heart. She tried not to show it, though. Something about Kira reminded Tanya of a wild bird, skittish and quick to retreat if she thought you were getting too comfortable.

Back in the kitchen, Tanya explained what acids and bases were, and she showed Kira how the cabbage water could change colors depending on what it was mixed with. The little girl poured some of the purple water into a glass with the vinegar, turning the mixture a brilliant pink. "This is my favorite color," she gushed.

"That's my friend Maggie's favorite color, too," Tanya said.

"Does she live here?" Kira asked.

Tanya poured some of the baking soda mixture into the bright pink glass. It bubbled a bit before turning the mixture purple again. "Yep. We've been friends since preschool."

Kira added in more of the baking soda mixture,

turning the contents of the glass a deep forest green. She seemed to wilt a bit. "I miss my friends."

"I bet they miss you, too," Tanya said. She imagined that Kira must be awfully lonely at Mrs. Fogelman's house, with her great-aunt so distracted and nobody else to talk to. "Are you making any new friends at your school up here?"

Kira shook her head. "I'm not going to school up here. Since it's only for a few weeks, my school back home sends me packets of work to do, and Auntie Dot sends them back when I'm done."

"Got it," Tanya said. She watched Kira's face, worried that talk of her friends back home would put her into one of her unhappy moods again. Maybe she should change the subject. "So, are you ready to start cleaning up?" Kira nodded, and Tanya helped her pour the mixtures down the sink. "Maybe I could invite Maggie to come over with me sometime, if your great-aunt says it's all right. We could have a little party."

"Okay," Kira said. "And maybe you and Maggie can bring your dolls over, too, and we can play with them upstairs."

Tanya's hands trembled as she poured the last of the cabbage water down the sink. "Sure. But I thought you didn't like the doll room."

Kira scraped the limp cabbage leaves into the compost bin under the sink. "I didn't at first, but now I do. Mary Rose makes it fun."

Tanya didn't say anything as she put the other ingredients back into her bag. She still couldn't quite let herself believe that Kira's new favorite toy was the same doll from her nightmares. How was something like that even possible? It couldn't be. Maybe Tanya's dream had come from seeing the doll in a picture somewhere without remembering it, or maybe Mrs. Fogelman had talked about it with Tanya's parents sometime, and Tanya had half overheard.

Kira was a lonely little kid, and her great-aunt had given her a special toy to keep her company. There was no way Tanya was going to let her own unfounded fears ruin that. After all, she was a scientist, wasn't she? There was obviously a logical explanation, and if she didn't know what it was, then it was her job to find out.

. . . . .

The next morning at school, Tanya zipped up her canvas backpack and straightened an enamel robot pin that had come loose from where she had attached it to the front pocket. Her eyes were puffy, and she stifled another yawn. She had had the nightmare again last night, exactly the same as the other dreams, and she had been too afraid to go back to sleep. Instead, she had read Ethan's book and studied the shards again, hoping to uncover something new, but neither elicited anything they could use against the Night Queen.

She looked over at the others, wondering if she should tell them about her fear. Rebecca crouched next to her, tying the laces of her retro Adidas high-tops. Clio checked her locker mirror and put on a light coat of coral-tinted lip balm. Maybe instead of telling them outright, Tanya could just bring the subject up hypothetically, act like it was just an idea she had thought of. That was probably better than saying, *Hey, by the way, this doesn't make any sense, but I dreamed about an evil doll and now I think that doll is in the house where I'm babysitting.* After all, it's not like anything had actually happened. She would just mention it casually. No specifics.

Tanya had just opened her mouth to speak when Maggie careened down the hall, nearly colliding with Rebecca when she reached the lockers. "I lost my phone. Am I late?"

Rebecca checked her watch. "Nope, we still have at least seven minutes." Tanya did the mental calculations. It would be weird to bring anything up right before everyone had to rush off to class, but seven minutes would be enough time to make it sound like she was asking an idle question, just one of the many bizarre things they were always talking about.

She shoved her hands in the pockets of her faded black jeans and leaned against her locker, hoping to look casual. "So I was doing some research last night, and—" she tried to make her voice sound light and carefree, as though she had just thought of something.

Maggie tapped Tanya's arm. "Hey, T, can you move? You're blocking my locker."

"Oh, sorry." Tanya scooted aside. "So, anyway, I was wondering . . . do you think—"

"Oh, hey, Ethan." Rebecca waved as Ethan sidled up in a moss-green plaid flannel and jeans. "Good shirt; it makes your eyes look really blue."

"Thanks," Ethan said. He peeked under his lashes at Clio, who was suddenly very busy organizing her backpack. "Hi, Clio."

"Oh, hi!" Clio said, as though she hadn't been periodically checking the hall for him since the girls had arrived this morning. She picked a tiny piece of lint off the orange tights she wore under a vintage bell-sleeve trapeze dress. "Did you find that other source you needed for your history project last night?"

Ethan grinned and nodded. "It definitely helps having a mom who's the Piper reference librarian."

"Speaking of last night—" Tanya tried again.

Maggie wailed, "Oh, not again!"

"What happened?" Clio asked.

"I left my English essay at home!" Maggie let out a frustrated growl. "Seriously! Why do teachers insist on torturing us with stupid homework to ruin our lives?"

Rebecca slipped her backpack onto her shoulders. "Oh, I don't know, maybe teach us valuable skills like organization, planning, and time management?" She laughed and danced away as Maggie swatted at her.

Tanya watched her friends, feeling strangely invisible. Sure, it was right before class when everyone was busy and distracted, but what she had to say was important, too, wasn't it? *But if it was really that important, wouldn't you have told them last night instead of trying to bring it up in casual conversation?* Tanya shoved her hands deeper in her pockets and slouched down the hall after the others. The truth is, she didn't know what the doll dreams meant. She only knew that for the first time in her life, she felt truly afraid.

CHAPTER
7

TANYA FELT A tiny sliver of anxiety as she rang the bell at Mrs. Fogelman's that afternoon. Would it be the sunshiny, happy Kira today, or the sullen, angry Kira who wanted nothing to do with her? She held her breath as the door opened, and when it was Mrs. Fogelman who answered, Tanya had a feeling that this wouldn't be a great babysitting day.

"Oh, Tanya, I almost forgot you were coming today," Mrs. Fogelman said.

Tanya wasn't quite sure how to answer that. "Um, okay, well, I'm here." She gave what she hoped was a warm smile and waited to be invited in. But Mrs. Fogelman just stood there, staring at her like she couldn't quite understand what the babysitter was still doing on her front porch. Tanya cleared her throat. "So, is Kira upstairs?" She peered past the older woman's shoulder into the house, hoping that would encourage her to move things along.

Mrs. Fogelman shook her head like she was clearing away cobwebs. "Yes. Right. We had lunch together in the sunroom around noon, and then she headed upstairs to play for a while." She squinted up at the gray sky. "What time is it now?"

"It's three thirty," Tanya said patiently. "The time you asked me to come."

"Three thirty already? My, the time does fly, doesn't it?" Bracelets rattling, she finally ushered Tanya inside. "Well, come along in and make yourself at home. You know where everything is, don't you?" Without waiting for an answer, Mrs. Fogelman drifted toward the back door. "I'll be in my studio." The back door was already closing behind her. "My masterpiece awaits!" she called over her shoulder.

Tanya stood alone in the silent house, staring after Mrs. Fogelman. "Okay, then," she said to the empty room. She put her bag down on the floor. "Time to get upstairs and find Kira." Her feet didn't move. She knew where she would find Kira. "I'll go get her in a second," she said quietly. "But maybe I'll set up in the kitchen first." Tanya picked up her bag and carried it to the back of the house. She had no idea why she was talking out loud to herself, but something about hearing her own ordinary, matter-of-fact voice brought a feeling of normalcy to the tense, anxious silence that hung in the air.

Tanya had brought one of her old science kits she had gotten for Christmas a few years back. It was a circuitry set, and she knew Kira would be excited to figure out how to clip the wires together to turn on the kit's tiny lightbulb. But when she went to unpack her bag on the counter, Tanya was surprised to discover that the kitchen was a mess. Mrs. Fogelman usually kept everything tidy and put away, but today the dirty lunch dishes were piled up in the sink, and several of the cabinet doors were open. Tanya guessed they had made hamburgers for lunch, because an empty Styrofoam tray sat in a sticky ring of dried meat juice near the dish rack. Her lip curled as she peeled it from the counter and dumped it in the recycling bin. She could still smell the blood that was congealing in the tray's corner. How anyone would want to eat something like that was beyond her.

Tanya took her time loading the dishwasher and wiping everything clean before setting up the kit. *Kira and I need a clean workspace for the project, so I may as well get it ready before she comes down*, she told herself, scrubbing extra hard at a stubborn bit of dried ketchup on the counter. *That's why I'm doing it now. It's not because I'm afraid to go upstairs.* She noticed the darkening sky outside, and she picked up her pace. January in Oregon meant the sun set before five, and Tanya felt a sudden sense of urgency. She didn't like thinking of Kira alone up in the doll room after dark.

That's ridiculous, Tanya thought. *A room is a room whether it's day or night.* Nevertheless, she hurried upstairs, flipping on lights as she went. Her legs felt heavier the closer she got to the doll room, but she ignored the feeling. "It's no big deal, Tanya," she whispered to herself. "So you're gonna see a bunch of spooky, gross dolls, and then you're gonna go back downstairs. That's it. Nothing to freak out about. Dolls. Can't. Do. Anything."

She pushed down the last of the worries and fears that threatened to bubble back up and pasted a smile on her face as she opened the door and switched on the light. "Hey, Kira! I have such a cool experiment set up downstairs!"

Kira turned and blinked at the sudden brightness. Her blond hair was tousled, and her pale eyes looked round and owlish when they met Tanya's. "Oh. Hi. I didn't know you were coming today." She turned around and went back to tending her doll, which was seated across from Kira in a chair at the little table.

Tanya couldn't quite read the little girl's mood. This definitely wasn't the sunny Kira, but it didn't seem like the ornery Kira, either. "What are you playing with Mary Rose today?"

"I'm feeding her," Kira said faintly, her voice colorless and flat. She dipped a little silver spoon into a tiny china bowl, and the sound was so familiar that it made Tanya want to scream.

"Cool. Maybe you could take a break and feed her later so we can go downstairs and get started on our project?"

Kira dropped the empty spoon into the bowl with a clatter, and Tanya swallowed thickly. "It's okay," Kira said. "She's finished."

"Great." Tanya tried to hide the relief in her voice. "Do the bowl and spoon need to be put away downstairs, or do they stay up here?"

"I just told you I *fed* her," Kira snapped. "Everybody knows you don't leave dirty dishes upstairs. You take them downstairs to be *washed*." She picked them up and stalked over to Tanya, shoving the little bowl and spoon into her hand.

Tanya hid a smile. This sounded much more like the Kira she was used to. "You got it. When we get to the kitchen, you can show me where to put them in the dishwasher." She shifted the dishes in her hand

and winced when her fingers touched something wet and sticky. They *were* dirty. She looked down to find a small red film lining the bowl. She caught a hint of the same scent she had smelled downstairs. *Blood.* Her vision swam and she leaned weakly against the wall in the hallway, pressing her head against the cool plaster.

Kira switched off the light and pulled the door closed behind her. "Good night, Mary Rose," she called softly. Her voice dropped to a whisper. "And don't worry, my sweet. I'll have more for you tomorrow."

· · · · ·

Tanya was on autopilot as she followed Kira downstairs and wordlessly handed her the little bowl and spoon to put in the dishwasher. She passed a towel after they both washed their hands, and then she pulled a banana out of the fruit bowl in the middle of the table. "You must be hungry. Why don't you have a snack for a sec? I'll be right back."

Without waiting for an answer, Tanya walked straight to the bathroom and locked herself in. For a moment, she thought she might throw up, but the feeling passed, and she splashed water on her face with trembling hands. She stared at her reflection in the mirror. *This is more than just some irrational fear,* she thought. *I don't know what exactly is going on here, but there's definitely something wrong.*

Without hesitation, she pulled out her phone and sent a group text to the girls, Kawanna, and Ethan.

[Tanya 3:45 PM] Big problem Creature Features tomorrow before school?

[Rebecca 3:45 PM] What's wrong? U OK?

[Maggie 3:45 PM] OMG WHAT HAPPENED?!?!?!

[Clio 3:45 PM] U still babysitting? Want us to come over?

[Tanya 3:45 PM] Can't explain now 7 AM?

[Maggie 3:46 PM] OK. Your the worst tho

[Rebecca 3:46 PM] *you're*

[Maggie 3:46 PM] Priorities! Tanya is in GRAVE DANGER and your focusing on my grammar?

[Rebecca 3:46 PM] *you're* 😈

That brought a small smile to Tanya's face. Just knowing her friends were there for her made her feel instantly calmer. Her phone buzzed again.

[Ethan 3:47 PM] I'll be there. I hear there's doughnuts? 😉

[Kawanna 3:47 PM] DON'T PUSH YOUR LUCK ETHAN

[Kawanna 3:47 PM]

[Kawanna 3:47 PM] But someone please bring caffeine!

[Ethan 3:47 PM] I got you covered

Tanya put her phone back in her pocket and looked again at her reflection in the mirror. Her normally tan skin had a waxen cast, and her eyes were glassy and feverish. Her mom would probably say she seemed *a little green around the gills*. She gripped the edges of the sink and took a deep breath. "Get it together, girl," she whispered. "You've seen scarier stuff than this, and you barely even blinked. You got this." But the girl in the mirror didn't look like she believed a word of it.

CHAPTER 8

THE SUN WASN'T yet past the horizon when Tanya and the others met the next morning in Kawanna's office at the back of Creature Features. A box of doughnuts sat in the middle of the lacquered coffee table next to a silver tray with a fresh pot of jasmine tea, and Kawanna and the kids quietly got settled with their early morning breakfast as they waited to hear what Tanya had to say. Tanya picked at her doughnut and looked at the circle of expectant faces, struggling to choose the right words to explain. But how was she supposed to fill her friends in on what was happening when she still didn't know what was going on herself?

It was Kawanna who spoke first. She was cocooned in her bright-blue-and-vermilion bathrobe, her dreadlocks were wrapped in a silk scarf, and her fuzzy green monster slippers nestled together on the floor in front of her. "There must be something pretty serious going on if you got us up this early, so spill it, girl. We're listening." She took a long sip of the tall cup of chai Ethan had brought for her.

Tanya took a deep breath and dived in, telling her friends about the nightmares, Mrs. Fogelman's doll collection, and Kira's strange behavior with Mary Rose.

Clio put her jelly doughnut back on her plate. "That *is* super weird." She wiped the powdered sugar off her fingers with a napkin. "It definitely has to be more than a coincidence."

Tanya picked up her teacup. "But I'm not *sure* the doll winked at me. I mean, what could possibly cause that? It may have just been my imagination. To be honest, every doll has me so scared at this point that I can't even tell anymore."

"I know what you mean," Maggie said. "After I first saw *Poltergeist*, I got so freaked out I was sure I could see the tree outside my window coming to get me." She looked around the room. "It totally wasn't, though."

"Yeah, we got that," Rebecca said.

"Even if the winking part *was* just your imagination, I agree there's something bigger going on either way," Clio said. "Those are some pretty specific details to dream about and then see them happen in real life."

"Hold up, though," Rebecca interjected. "Kira was definitely *feeding blood* to the doll? You're positive about that?"

Tanya nodded. "Just like in my dream."

Maggie pulled off a piece of her pink frosted doughnut. "What kind of blood was it? It wasn't, like, human or anything, was it?"

"I don't think so," Tanya said. "I asked Kira about it, and she said it was left over from the hamburger meat they had for lunch."

"Well, that makes the situation about one percent less terrifying, I guess," Maggie said. "At least it wasn't from a living thing."

"Cows *are* living things," Tanya said.

"Oh, come on," Maggie retorted. "You know what I mean. It's not like Kira went out and killed a cow herself."

"Can we just go back to the part where she fed the doll?" Rebecca asked. "You said the bowl was empty when Kira handed it to you, right?"

"Uh-huh," Tanya agreed, "but there had been something in it before."

"Right," Rebecca said. "So where did the blood go?"

"What do you mean?" Maggie asked. "She said Kira gave it to the doll."

"Yeah, I know," Rebecca replied. She held up her teacup. "But say I had a cup of tea, and I wanted to feed it to that cat statue." She pointed to the gold maneki-neko statue Kawanna had on the bookshelves behind her desk. "What would happen if I tried to pour this tea into its mouth?"

Ethan's face brightened. "I get it. It would spill everywhere."

"Right," Rebecca said. "It's not like the cat statue can really drink it, so there's nowhere for the tea to go." She put her teacup back down. "So unless you saw blood spilled all over the place, it must have gone somewhere."

Tanya paled. "I can't believe I didn't think of that." She pulled her knees up into her lap and hugged them. "Does that mean that Mary Rose really might have come alive somehow, just like in my dream?" A wave of dizziness washed over her. "I don't feel so well."

Kawanna stood up and put a warm hand on Tanya's shoulder. "I know how frightened you must be, but remember, you're still a scientist." Her voice was kind, and she looked into Tanya's face until she saw Tanya's eyes meet hers. "And what do scientists do when faced with something they can't explain?"

Tanya felt comforted by Kawanna's steadying gaze. "They start by trying to rule out any logical explanations." She nodded slowly. "Okay. I can do that."

"Of course you can," Maggie said. "It's, like, one of your favorite things to do."

"Brainstorming time! I'll make a list," Rebecca volunteered.

Tanya handed over her notebook. "Write it in here."

Rebecca clicked her mechanical pencil. "Okay, ready. What have we got?"

Everyone was quiet for a moment, thinking. "I have an idea," Maggie said. "Do you guys remember that baby doll I had in kindergarten? It had an open mouth, and they sold these little packets of food you could mix so you could actually feed it."

"I remember that," Rebecca said. "Didn't you end up having to throw it away because you forgot to clean it and it got all moldy inside?"

Maggie waved her hand dismissively. "That's beside the point." She leaned forward and pointed to the notebook. "But Mary Rose could be one of those kinds of dolls, right? That would explain the disappearing blood. Put that on the list." Rebecca diligently made it the first bullet point.

"I don't think it's like that," Tanya said slowly. "This doll seemed really old." She shivered. "With its creepy porcelain face and weird sausage-curl hair."

"Yeah, but I'm sure my doll wasn't the first to be the kind you can feed, right?" Maggie said.

"That's right," Kawanna said. "Even as far back as the 1930s there were dolls that worked like that. My mother used to talk about her first Betsy Wetsy doll. She said you could give it bottles of water and then later change its diapers."

"So it was basically a doll that just peed all the time?" Maggie asked, mystified. "Why would anyone want a peeing doll?"

Rebecca piped in. "So. Action item: research the doll. Get a closer look. Find out its history. Got it. Okay, what else?"

Ethan looked down and toyed with the hem of his black T-shirt. "There's still the possibility that the doll *is* actually haunted by something," he said quietly.

"You're right," Rebecca said. She added *haunted doll* to the list. "Is there a way to test that? Some experiment we could do?" She looked at Tanya. When Tanya didn't say anything, Rebecca prodded her gently. "What about that book that Ethan lent you? Maybe there's something in there?"

Tanya's mind felt slow and mushy. A part of her had been hoping her friends would tell her that all of her fears were just in her imagination. That there was no way the dreams could possibly have any link to her babysitting. But instead, here they were, making lists like a doll coming to life was a totally plausible thing to happen. Was everything she had ever learned about the world just totally meaningless? Were there really no rules at all? She closed her eyes. It was all too much.

Clio and her aunt exchanged a look. "Let's forget Kira and the doll for a second. When did you start having these bad dreams?"

"A few weeks ago," Tanya answered. "I don't remember the exact date, but I recorded them all in the notebook."

Rebecca flipped through the pages, scanning each one quickly. "It looks like it was just under two weeks ago." Her eyes narrowed as she took a closer look at Tanya's notes. "In between your entries about the dreams you have a lot of notes about the shards we found from the Night Queen's mirror. Did your dreams begin at the same time you started investigating the mirror?"

"No," Tanya said. "I've been studying the mirror pieces since before Christmas, but the dreams started more recently."

"Hmm," Kawanna said. "And the Night Queen isn't in any of your dreams?"

"No," Tanya replied. "That's the weird part. The two don't seem to be connected at all."

"I mean, there has to be *some* kind of connection," Clio said. "It's just too much of a coincidence otherwise." She paused and took a bite of her jelly doughnut while she thought. "Has anything strange happened with the mirror? Even something little, like you caught a flash of something, or one of your experiments had an unexpected result?"

"The only unexpected thing is that I haven't discovered anything from the shards at all, not even when I thought I would. A rock would react more than those stupid mirror pieces."

"Well, let's put it on the list anyway." Rebecca added it to the list of bullet points in the notebook. "I don't like the idea of those shards sitting around where someone can find them," she added. "Sure, they haven't done anything so far, but I still think they could be dangerous." She grimaced. "And they've been in your room for more than a month. If I had something of the Night Queen's in my room for that long, I bet I would start having nightmares, too."

"Yeah, I think we should get rid of them just to be on the safe side," Clio agreed.

"How?" Maggie asked. "It's not like we can just throw them in the trash or something."

Clio looked at Ethan. "Any ideas?"

"Maybe," Ethan said. "I gotta do some more research."

Kawanna stood up. "While you're at school today, I'll check the books in Miss Pearl's collection here and see what I can find." She stacked the empty teacups and picked up the silver tea tray. "So, do we have a plan?"

Rebecca looked back at her notes. "Mostly. We'll see what we can find out about this Mary Rose doll, check out Ethan's collection of books about haunted stuff, and research anything we can find about how to properly dispose of an evil mirror. So, as much as that can be considered a plan, then I guess we have a plan."

Maggie made a face. "Why do our plans always seem to involve reading? Can't we ever have a plan that makes us go shopping? Or give someone a make-over? Nope, it's always just dusty old books!"

"There *is* something I need help with, and it has nothing to do with books," Tanya said.

Maggie leaned forward. "Ooh, what is it?"

"I don't really want to babysit at Mrs. Fogelman's house by myself anymore," Tanya began. The others nodded in agreement. "And Kira's a little bit more of a girly-girl type than I am. And she's kind of hard to read sometimes. I told her all about you, and she wants to meet you. Maybe you could come with me the next time I babysit?"

Maggie looked surprised. "You want *me* to come help?"

"Well, yeah," Tanya said. "You know I'm not the most outgoing person in the world. And you're always the one who makes us laugh, so you're the perfect person to help get Kira out of her shell. And maybe distract her from Mary Rose." Tanya stood and picked up her backpack. "And also, like, investigate Mary Rose. Because I still don't want to go near that thing."

Maggie shrugged. "Works for me. I still have, like, a million American Girl dolls, so how scary can one more doll be?"

Tanya's smile was grim. "Trust me. You have no idea."

CHAPTER
9

MAGGIE AND TANYA checked their phones one more time as they walked down the sidewalk to Mrs. Fogelman's house. It was a raw, soggy afternoon, and both girls had wool hats pulled down tightly over their ears. Droplets of water clung to the red curls that spilled out of Maggie's fluffy angora beanie, and Tanya's breath came out in clouds from between the folds of the scarf she had pulled up over her nose to keep it from going numb.

"Ethan and Rebecca are checking Moina's old papers to look for anything about haunted dolls, and Clio and Kawanna are seeing what they can find out about getting rid of the mirror," Tanya reported as she read from her screen.

"Cool," Maggie said. "We can leave all that boring

junk to them, while we get all the fun stuff. What if the doll's eyes go all red, and it's like, 'YOU WILL NOT LEAVE THIS HOUSE ALIVE'? That's what always happens in the movies."

"Don't joke about that," Tanya said, surprised at the sharpness in her voice. Having Maggie with her did feel better, but it wasn't enough to take Tanya's fear away.

"Sorry," Maggie said. "I'm just trying to lighten the mood."

"No, I'm sorry for snapping at you. It's not your fault," Tanya said. "It's just that nothing has ever really scared me before, and I guess I don't like it."

"Well, I'm scared pretty much always, and joking about it is actually one of the things that keeps me from running away screaming most of the time."

Tanya nodded thoughtfully. "Okay. Good to know." She tapped Maggie on the arm. "Hey, we should get some pictures of Mary Rose, too. We might be able to use them to find out more about where she came from."

"Got it." Suddenly Maggie brightened. "I have an idea! Maybe we could pretend we have to do a research project on heirlooms for our history class, and we can ask Mrs. Fogelman to tell us about how the doll came into her family."

"That's not a bad plan," Tanya said. "If we can

get Mrs. Fogelman to sit down long enough to talk to us. She basically jets straight out to her studio the second I arrive."

"Well, that's because she hasn't met *me* yet," Maggie quipped. "I am a profoundly charming individual, you know!"

Tanya laughed. "You wish!" She opened the front gate and led Maggie up the steps to the porch.

Mrs. Fogelman opened the door almost immediately. "Perfect timing! I was just telling Kira that you would be arriving any minute." Her silver-streaked hair was twisted into a braid and coiled at the nape of her neck, and she wore a handmade, plum-colored poncho over paint-splattered jeans. She was barefoot.

"Great," Tanya answered. "This is my friend Maggie. I told you she'd be coming with me today. She's a baby-sitter, too."

Mrs. Fogelman shook Maggie's hand, gripping it tightly. Maggie winced as the artist's silver and turquoise rings dug into her fingers. "It's lovely to meet you," Mrs. Fogelman said. "What beautiful hair you have, like a girl in a Renoir painting." She reached out and touched Maggie's curls. Maggie shot Tanya a secret *See, I told you so!* smirk, and Tanya grinned. "Do come in," Mrs. Fogelman continued. "I'm sure Kira will be thrilled to have another friend around, especially with so many demands on my time tonight." She picked up a flyer from the side table near the door and handed it to Tanya. "I'm attending a poetry reading this evening at the library, and Kira absolutely refused to come along. I'll leave straight from my studio around six, and I should be home by ten."

Tanya nodded and took the flyer.

Maggie trailed her hand lightly along the top of the sofa, taking in the decor of the house. "Wow, you have so many cool collections." Maggie craned her neck to follow the line of seashells on the walls near the ceiling. "Tanya says you're an artist. Do you use parts of your collections in your art?"

"It's funny you should ask that," Mrs. Fogelman replied. "The sculpture I'm working on is a freestanding mosaic that's a combination of collection pieces and found objects. Would you like to see it?"

Maggie raised her eyebrows, and her gaze quickly met Tanya's. "Sure," they both said at once. Maybe the two girls could get Mrs. Fogelman to tell them more about Mary Rose while they toured her studio.

Mrs. Fogelman stopped at the bottom of the staircase. "Kira!" she called up. "I'm taking the girls to my studio out back. Would you like to join us?"

There was a pause. Finally, a faint *No* could be heard drifting down the stairs. Mrs. Fogelman shrugged and stroked the silver and amber pendant around her neck. "Kids," she said simply, and breezed down the hallway to the back door.

Just as Mrs. Fogelman was about to step outside, Tanya stopped her. "Don't you want shoes?" Mrs. Fogelman stared at her uncomprehendingly for a moment. Tanya pointed at the artist's bare feet. "It's cold outside."

"Well, it's only a short walk, but I suppose you're right," Mrs. Fogelman agreed. She pulled on a battered pair of ankle-length red cowboy boots and walked into the soggy yard, squelching through the muddy turf. "The sculpture is nearly finished," she said when they reached the bright blue door in the studio's brown-shingled facade. She turned back and pointed to a dirt-streaked tarpaulin in the yard. "I'm going to put it there, where the fish pond used to be." She pulled out a set of keys and unlocked the door. "I never had any luck with that dreadful pond. I couldn't seem to keep those fish alive, the poor dears. I would come out in the morning and find them belly-up in the lily pads. Eli was sure there must be a fungus in the water or some kind of disease, so we finally just tore it out."

The girls followed Mrs. Fogelman into the studio, and both couldn't help gasping when they saw the light-soaked space. The studio was a converted garage, and Mrs. Fogelman had replaced the original garage door with one that was made of frosted glass. Several skylights in the roof ensured that the room was bathed in a diffuse silvery light, even in the late afternoon of an overcast winter's day. More of Mrs. Fogelman's wild paintings leaned against the walls in stacks, and a variety of mosaic sculpture pieces stood nearby. A twirling metal mobile hung from the ceiling, the winglike pieces covered in bright coats of enamel.

There were several twisted metal sculptures clustered together in a corner near a large oil painting of a bleak winter landscape. They looked very different from the other work in the room, and Maggie cautiously touched one. "Those were Eli's," Mrs. Fogelman explained. "He left them to me when he died last month. We had very different artistic styles, but we loved collaborating. I still can't believe he's gone."

"I'm so sorry," Tanya said.

Mrs. Fogelman's eyes filled with tears, but she waved them away. "Motorcycle accident. But that was my Eli, always a reckless one. He wouldn't have it any other way." She walked to the center of the room, where a canvas drop cloth covered something that was roughly the size of a small fountain. "This was our final collaboration, and I've almost completed it. I just need to mount this inside the basin and add a few finishing touches." She bent over and reached both hands into a wooden crate to retrieve a black glass orb with a milky sheen. "Isn't it marvelous? It's an antique gazing globe Eli found at an estate sale in town." She returned the globe to the crate and looked up at the girls. "I can think of no better way to honor Eli's memory than to complete the work we began together." She swept the drop cloth off the sculpture with a flourish. "I call it *Unburied Past*."

The sculpture was made of twisted metal and concrete that swirled and curved upward to support a shallow stone basin with a deep recess in the center. Although it still wasn't finished, much of it was already encrusted with chips of mosaic tile and mirror bits that reflected blue, silver, and creamy white. Shiny black metal wove through it in molten veins that seemed at once to catch the light and drink it in. Tanya knew enough about art to understand that what she was looking at was something extraordinary. "It's beautiful," she said, but she found that she didn't really mean it. In fact, something about the artwork repulsed her. Tanya didn't carry strong opinions about art either way, so she wondered what it was that she found so unappealing.

She took a step closer and studied the sculpture. Then she realized what bothered her. The twisting base was sculpted to look like grasping arms, rising up from the earth and clawing at the stone bowl. It made her think of the rotting arms of the *lusus naturae* bursting from the ground and grasping at the girls, trying to pull them back through to the Nightmare Realm. She cast a sideways glance at Maggie, wondering what she thought of it.

"This is amazing," Maggie said. "Why aren't you going to sell it? That's how artists make a living, right?"

Mrs. Fogelman ran a hand lovingly over the sculpture. "Ah, that's the curse of being an artist. Every time you sell something, it's like giving up a part of yourself." She picked up the drop cloth and placed it gently back over the sculpture. "Sometimes pieces that I've sold come to visit me in dreams. Those were the ones I know I should have kept." Her eyes blazed, and she put a protective hand atop the covered work. "*Unburied Past* is far too precious to share. I could never part with it!" She moved her body to block it from the girls, as though she thought that one of them would try to take it from her.

Tanya's eyes met Maggie's. The artist was giving off an intense energy. "So I guess it will kind of become your own family heirloom to pass down," Maggie said finally. "That's neat. Kind of like the doll that you gave Kira. She said it used to belong to your aunt?"

Mrs. Fogelman's eyes looked fuzzy for a moment, and then they cleared. "Oh, you mean Mary Rose?" She chuckled. "Yes, that old doll has been passed down from aunt to niece for generations. My own niece, Amanda, wasn't much for dolls, of course, so I saved it for her daughter, Kira. If that doll could talk, what marvelous tales she would have to tell of all the adventures she's had with the little girls in my family."

"Aunt to niece, huh?" Maggie asked. "Why not mother to daughter?"

"It's a funny thing. None of us who inherited Mary Rose grew up to have any daughters of our own. No children at all, in fact. So it was a lucky thing we had Mary Rose." Mrs. Fogelman gazed into the distance, and her eyes grew cloudy with memory. "There were times when Mary Rose felt like the daughter I never had." She shook her head. "That must sound strange, I suppose."

Tanya felt the hairs on her arms stand on end, and she and Maggie looked at each other. "Um . . . no. Not at all," Tanya said slowly. Mrs. Fogelman was an adult. How could a *doll* feel like a daughter to her?

"I was so happy when Amanda had a little girl.

Otherwise the tradition would have died out completely, and that would be the end of Mary Rose."

"Wow," Maggie said. "How old is Mary Rose? Where did she come from?"

"Oh, goodness," Mrs. Fogelman said. "I'm not sure, exactly. The first little girl to have her was my great-great-great-aunt, Elee Stone. That must have been right around the town's founding, I suppose. The Stones were one of the town's most prominent families at the time. Her father had the doll made especially for her."

Tanya and Maggie exchanged another look. *Interesting.* "That's cool," Maggie said. "Are there any other stories in your family about Mary Rose?" Mrs. Fogelman tilted her head and stared at Maggie, her eyes narrowing slightly.

"If there are, I don't remember any of them," Mrs. Fogelman said briskly. "I loved Mary Rose dearly, but for the life of me I can't recall a single thing I used to do when I played with her." She opened the door and ushered the girls back outside. "Now, run along to the house! I'm sure Kira will be wondering where you've gotten off to." Before the girls could reply, they heard the studio door close and lock behind them.

CHAPTER 10

WHEN THE GIRLS got back to the house, they found Kira upstairs in the doll room. She was rocking Mary Rose in her arms and singing quietly to herself. She had pulled a high chair into the center of the room and seated a few rows of dolls in front of it. Tanya noticed an empty bowl and spoon on the little table in the corner, and her mouth went dry.

"Hey, Kira. This is my friend Maggie that I was telling you about."

Kira barely looked up. "Oh. Hi." She placed Mary Rose in the high chair and pointed it so it faced the rows of dolls on the floor.

"Tanya says your favorite color is hot pink, same as mine," Maggie tried.

"Yeah, I guess," Kira answered, her voice listless.

"I brought a really fun experiment to do," Tanya said, "and your auntie Dot said we can order pizza for dinner. Plus I brought a really cool book of stories we can read before you go to bed."

"Bedtime stories?" Kira scoffed. "I read Jasmine Toguchi books by myself all the time. I don't need anyone to read to me like I'm a baby."

"Okay, well, my dad still reads to me every night, and I'm in seventh grade," Tanya replied. "But it's fine if you don't want to."

Kira scowled. "Good. Because I *don't* want to." She picked up a little silver hairbrush. "I just want to stay here and play with Mary Rose."

"Is that Mary Rose?" Maggie asked. "I've heard a lot about her. She's so pretty. Can I hold her?"

Kira's eyes narrowed with suspicion, and she stepped protectively in front of the doll in the high chair, just like Mrs. Fogelman had done with the sculpture in her studio. "Why do you want to hold her?"

"I like dolls. I have a lot of them at home, too," Maggie said. She held out her hands, and Kira reluctantly passed her the doll. Mary Rose's cheeks looked pinker than Tanya remembered. Her blue eyes seemed brighter, her lips rosier. The rest of her was still as white as marble.

"Wow, she's so heavy," Maggie noted. "What's she made of?" She peeked under the doll's dress. "Oh, she has a cloth body." She turned it over and felt around the back. "It's kind of lumpy. Is there something else stitched in here?"

Kira snatched Mary Rose out of Maggie's arms. "You can't play with her anymore. She's *mine*."

"All right, you don't have to get huffy about it," Maggie said. She pulled out her phone. "How about if I take a picture of you and Mary Rose? It might be fun to send to your parents or your friends back home." Kira faced the camera and cradled the doll, her face stony. "Don't you want to smile or anything?" Kira just stared. Maggie took a few steps closer and zoomed in to snap a few close-ups of Mary Rose.

"I think Mary Rose looks tired," Tanya said. "Maybe we should let her take a nap while you play downstairs."

"You're just saying that because you don't like her," Kira muttered. She ran the silver brush over the doll's glossy golden hair.

"Well, *I* like her, and I think she looks tired, too." Maggie held out her hand. "Let's give her a rest, and we'll come back up later." She patted the daybed. "Should we put her right here so she has a comfy pillow?"

"No," Kira said. She slipped the doll into the high chair. "Mary Rose says she wants to be here." She looked at the dolls on the floor and adjusted the chair so it faced them exactly. Then she followed the two older girls out of the room.

Once downstairs, Kira's mood grew lighter, and soon she was laughing and joking with Tanya and Maggie as they wrote silly messages to one another in the invisible ink they had made out of lemon juice. Kira wolfed down her pizza at dinner, and when she heard that Maggie had a YouTube channel, she insisted on seeing every one of her videos.

"Is that Tanya in a chicken outfit?" she shrieked, pointing at the screen. Tanya's cheeks grew warm when she saw herself flapping and wiggling in the yellow costume.

"It sure is," Maggie answered with a smirk.

"Were you embarrassed?" Kira asked.

"I sure was," Tanya answered.

A short time later, Tanya snuck a look at her watch and breathed an inward sigh of relief. It was already bedtime, and Kira hadn't once asked to go back upstairs to the doll room. "Time to brush your teeth and change into pjs."

"Do I have to?" Kira whined.

"You do," Tanya answered. "But Maggie and I can come upstairs with you if you want."

"No, I can do it." Kira hopped off her stool at the kitchen counter and stretched. "I'm gonna wear my unicorn nightgown to bed. The unicorns have rainbow manes and gold horns."

"That sounds fabulous," Maggie said. "I can't wait to see it when you come back down."

Kira disappeared upstairs, and Tanya turned to Maggie. "You were awesome, Mags. I knew you were the perfect person for this. Thanks for being here; I didn't feel scared at all."

"Are you kidding? You don't have to thank me. It was super fun!" Maggie flipped her hair behind her shoulder. "But it's true that I am both awesome and perfect, so thanks for noticing." Tanya laughed, and Maggie pulled out her phone and scrolled through the pictures she had taken. "You had me all set to meet some kind of demon spawn, but everything went pretty smoothly. Mary Rose looks like a normal doll to me, and Kira's a cute kid."

Tanya looked at the pictures and shuddered. Mary Rose just looked so *lifelike*, somehow. "Everything seemed fine to me, too, but wasn't it kind of weird that Kira took the doll away from you when you wanted to see what was inside it? And how she got all possessive about even letting you hold Mary Rose in the first place?" She passed the phone back to Maggie.

Maggie sent the photos over to the others, along with what Mrs. Fogelman had told them about the doll's history. "I guess so, but I don't know, T. Lots of kids get weird and possessive about their toys. I don't think you've ever let me touch your chemistry set."

"A chemistry set is not a toy!" Tanya said. She caught herself and laughed. "What I meant is that it's dangerous. That's why I don't let you touch it."

Maggie shot her the side-eye. "Uh-huh."

Tanya tossed the squeezed lemons into the compost and closed the cabinet door. "Then it was probably my imagination after all, just like I thought at first." She rinsed the juicer in the sink and tucked it into the dishwasher. "I knew it! A haunted doll is just way too ridiculous to be true, right?"

"You're probably asking the wrong person," Maggie said. "After all, I believed in supernatural stuff way before we ever met the Night Queen." She gathered up the pizza plates and carried them over to the sink. "But my mom always says to listen to your gut. What is your gut telling you?"

"I'm a scientist," Tanya answered. "We don't draw

conclusions based on our guts; we base them on existing data."

"Yeah, but look at everything that's happened to us over the last few months. Isn't it possible that some things just can't be explained scientifically?"

"No." Tanya's voice was firm. "The world has rules. And one of those rules is that everything has to have a logical explanation. That's why we have methods and experiments. That's why we have math formulas. That's why we use evidence."

Maggie sighed. "Fine. So what does the evidence tell you, then?"

Tanya folded her arms. "Well, there isn't much," she admitted. "Mostly just the dreams."

"Maybe those really are just a coincidence?" Maggie said hopefully. "I mean, wouldn't it be great if, just once, *something* in this spooky town actually turned out to be normal?"

Tanya's face clouded with doubt. "Sherlock Holmes doesn't believe in coincidences. Besides, what about the blood? Where does the blood go?"

Maggie slumped. "Oh, yeah. I forgot about that. We'll have to get a closer look at that doll after Kira goes to sleep. I did feel something lumpy in there."

Tanya finished loading the dishwasher. "Where is Kira? She should have come back down by now."

She dried her hands on the dish towel. "Let's go get her settled in bed."

Kira wasn't in her bedroom. She wasn't in the doll room, either. Tanya heard Kira's voice drifting down the hallway, and she followed it to Mrs. Fogelman's bedroom. "Kira? I don't think your auntie Dot would want you in here."

There was no answer from inside the room, but Tanya could see a crack of light showing from under the door to the master bathroom. She opened the door to find Kira planted on the floor talking to Mary Rose. The little girl was dressed in her night-gown, and her hair was wet. A crumpled towel was piled in the corner, and a layer of baby powder cov-ered the floor. "Whoa, this is a total mess. What happened?"

"I always take a shower before bed," Kira answered.

Tanya surveyed the room's wreckage, mentally calculating how long it would take to clean every-thing up. "I thought you had your own bathroom."

Kira pointed to the shower. "I like Auntie Dot's shower better. It has a bench in it." She picked up Mary Rose, who was covered in powder. "Mary Rose likes it better, too. See? She likes to sit right here." She plopped the doll down on the vanity between the two sinks, and a cloud of powder puffed up and misted the mirror.

Maggie crowded in the doorway behind Tanya. "Whoa. What's with all the baby powder?"

"I get sweaty," Kira answered.

"Ooo-kay," Maggie answered. "Not gonna ask any more about that." She turned to Tanya. "What do we do?"

Tanya looked at her watch again. "It's already past Kira's bedtime. Let's just put her to bed, finish cleaning up the kitchen, and then we'll tackle the bathroom." She held out her hand. "Come on, Kira."

Kira stood up. "Can Mary Rose come?"

"No way," Maggie said. "We need to clean her up, too. Now come over here so we can de-powder you." Careful to stay in the doorway, Maggie and Tanya brushed Kira off as best they could.

Kira padded into the bedroom, leaving white footprints on the wood floor. "Hang on," Tanya said. She grabbed a hand towel and wiped down Kira's feet and the prints she had left. "That's better."

As Kira cuddled under the covers, her pinched face looked worried. "I'm sorry I made a mess," she said quietly. "Are you mad at me?"

"I'm not mad," Tanya replied. "It's just . . . I wish

you had asked first, or told us you might need help with the powder."

Kira's worried expression turned to a scowl. "But I *didn't* need help. I use baby powder all the time."

"Really." Maggie's voice was light. "And does it always end up all over the bathroom?" Kira turned her head and wouldn't say anything.

Tanya sighed. She wished she could have just one nice babysitting day without Kira getting all prickly. "Well, even though we have a lot of mess to clean up, I still had a fun time with you." She stood up and switched off the hula-girl lamp. Kira didn't answer, and Tanya and Maggie tiptoed into the hall. Tanya turned back. "Do you want me to leave the door open?"

"Why? Because I might be scared like some baby?" Kira demanded. "You can shut it. I'm not afraid of the dark."

Tanya struggled to keep her patience. "Okay, then. I'll go ahead and close it." She pulled the door closed but poked her head in one final time. "Good night, Kira."

Just as Tanya was turning away, she heard Kira's voice softly call out to her, "Good night. Thanks for a fun time."

. . . . .

Tanya finished wiping down the kitchen countertops and put the pizza box into the recycling bin while Maggie swept the floor. "Okay, now I kind of get what you mean about Kira," Maggie said quietly. "Is she always so hot-and-cold like that?"

"Pretty much," Tanya said. "I think she was a little better with you here. You have more of a sparkly kind of personality than I do, and I think Kira's a kid who needs someone sparkly to draw her out."

Maggie fluttered her eyelashes. "Sparkly? Wow! Nobody's ever described me as sparkly before."

"Oh, come off it," Tanya said with a laugh. "You know you're a superstar."

"Well, yeah," Maggie said, "but now I'm a sparkly superstar!" She dumped the contents of the dustpan into the trash. "Should we head upstairs and tackle the bathroom?"

Tanya checked her watch. "We should have enough time to get it cleaned up before Mrs. Fogelman gets home. But I should probably still tell her what happened so she can talk to Kira about it. I don't want to be cleaning up a room full of baby powder every time I have to put Kira to bed."

"Totally," Maggie said. "It's going to take forever. But hey, maybe it won't be as bad as it looked at first."

"Doubtful."

They walked upstairs, and Tanya cast a glance at Kira's closed door. "I should check on her." She opened the door and peeked inside, the light from the hallway illuminating Kira's sleeping face. Next to her on the pillow was another, smaller face—white as marble, with wide blue eyes and a dusting of powder dulling the gleam of the flaxen hair.

"Ugh, are you kidding me?" Tanya whispered. She closed the door. "Kira must have gotten up and brought Mary Rose to bed with her. There's going to be powder all over the place."

She turned back to Maggie and found her face was as white as cheese, her green eyes wide with horror. "Kira didn't get up and take Mary Rose to bed."

"What do you mean? I saw her right in there!"

"Look." Maggie pointed at the floor where tiny white footprints trailed down the hallway from Mrs. Fogelman's room. Footprints the size of a doll's.

CHAPTER
11

TANYA BARELY SLEPT that night. She kept playing the events over and over in her head, seeing those tiny footprints stark white against the floor. By the time the sun crept over the horizon, she was already counting the minutes until everyone would meet up at Creature Features.

Rebecca and Clio looked crisp and purposeful when Tanya arrived. They bustled about the shop, setting up the doughnuts, tea, and the cinnamon rolls Rebecca had made earlier that morning. Even Kawanna seemed chipper, eschewing her usual morning pajamas for a teal jumpsuit and gold cuff bracelet. But Maggie looked just as rough as Tanya felt, with dark circles under her eyes, and her outfit lacking its usual flair. She had on a faded Joan Jett T-shirt and a pair of old pink sweats. Ethan came out of the back hallway carrying Kawanna's jadeite dessert plates and a handful of napkins. He grinned when he saw Tanya. "Hey, how did it go last night?"

"No talking about it until we've all got our doughnuts," Maggie said. "I need sugar to sustain me."

"That bad, huh?" Rebecca popped a pink frosted doughnut on one of the green plates and handed it to Maggie.

"You are a goddess," Maggie said, and took a bite, closing her eyes to savor the flavor. Rebecca laughed.

A few minutes later, everyone was slouched in the beanbag chairs Kawanna had pulled out, and all eyes were on Tanya. "Well, we've confirmed that it wasn't just my imagination like I'd hoped," she finally said. "That doll is definitely alive. Or possessed. Or something." Tanya told them about the footprints in the powder, Kira's strange obsession with Mary Rose, and the mysterious lump Maggie had felt in the doll's cloth body. The others' expressions grew grimmer as they listened.

"Did you find out anything about the Stone family or where they got the doll in the first place?" Tanya asked.

Ethan passed out a copy of an old newspaper article dated April 17, 1885. The headline said *Piper*

Women's Club Celebrates New Building with Tea Party for Local Girls. The photo showed several little girls with dolls in their laps, sitting around a tea set on a child-sized table. Tanya immediately recognized Mary Rose in the arms of a thin little girl with light skin and pale eyes. "That must be Elee," she said, pointing. Elee wore a dress with puffy sleeves and a lacy collar, and her plain hair was pulled back from her face with a ribbon.

"Elee's doll gets mentioned in the article, since hers wasn't store-bought like the others," Ethan said. "Elee's mom, Lily, gets a little braggy about it. Listen to this: *'My husband, Dr. Matthew Stone, commissioned the great Emmanuel Marquis to create Mary Rose especially for Elee's eighth birthday. This beautiful doll is truly a treasure that will be passed down for many generations to come.'*"

"Who's Emmanuel Marquis?" Maggie asked. "Is he supposed to be famous or something?" She reached for the breakfast platter and loaded a cinnamon roll onto her plate.

Rebecca pulled a manila folder out of her bag and opened it up. "Well, Ethan and I did a bit of digging, and it's kind of a familiar story. Emmanuel Marquis made his start running a small puppet theater on Main Street, and he made all his own puppets." Rebecca pulled out a copy of an old newspaper ad for the Marquis Puppet Theater. *Wonders and Enchantments!* it promised in text below a drawing of two grinning marionettes.

"Okay, no thanks," Clio said, grimacing at the ad. She shook her head and took a bite of her cinnamon roll.

"I guess everyone back then agreed with you, because the puppet show failed after just a few months," Rebecca continued. "Then Marquis went on to work in a pharmacy, but he got fired after he got caught stealing chemicals."

"What kind of chemicals?" Tanya asked.

"Sulfur, quicksilver, and a bunch of stuff I've never heard of," Rebecca went on. "He totally disappears from the town records for a while after that. Then all of a sudden, he shows up again a few years later. He came back to town to open an art studio. It was an instant success, and he made tons of money. He specialized in portraits and busts, and every rich family in town hired him to paint or sculpt them. You can still see some of his work in the library and town hall. He was a really big deal in Piper."

Kawanna took a long sip of her chai. "And that's why the Stone family decided to hire him to make Mary Rose for Elee?"

"If you were fancy, he would be the perfect person to hire for a one-of-a-kind doll," Rebecca said. "After all, he already knew how to make puppets, and once he was a famous artist, buying a doll from him would make anyone the talk of the town." Rebecca went on. "And Lily Stone was the kind of person who only wanted the best for her daughter, and she wouldn't take no for an answer, even though she knew that Emmanuel Marquis probably hated her husband."

"Why?" Tanya asked.

"Because Dr. Stone owned the pharmacy where Marquis worked," Ethan said. "He's the one who fired him."

"And get this," Rebecca added. "After Marquis sold the doll to the Stones, he closed up shop and left town."

"Where did he go?" Tanya asked.

Rebecca shrugged. "Nobody knows. We can't find a single record of him anywhere after that." She closed the folder and handed it to Kawanna, who tucked it away behind the counter.

"So Mary Rose was created by a chemical-stealing failed puppeteer with a grudge against the family he made her for? No wonder she's evil," Maggie said. "Do you think he, like, cursed her or something?"

"You know I don't believe in curses," Tanya said.

"But you do believe in the Night Queen," Rebecca said, "and I think this has the Night Queen written all over it. This is practically the same story as that theater guy."

"Graham Reynard Faust," Maggie interjected. "So you think Marquis was one of the Night Queen's minions, too, and Mary Rose is another of her nasty little creations?" Maggie asked. "Ugh, I thought we were finally done with her!"

Rebecca shook her head, her lips in a tight line. "We still aren't sure what the doll is for or what it can do. But the good news is it can't be that bad, right? After all, it's been passed down through the Stone family for more than a hundred years, and there were no big tragedies or disasters in the family history at all. No mysterious deaths. Nothing that would indicate the doll has any real power."

"Other than the power to come alive, you mean?" Tanya asked. She turned to Clio and Kawanna. "Did you two find anything about it here?"

"Nothing on Mary Rose," Kawanna said. "We looked for clues in Miss Pearl's old papers about the Night Queen. The last of her journals weren't exactly lucid. She wrote a lot about beacons and vessels, but her writing was so addled at the end that we're not sure what it means."

Clio leaned back and tented her hands. "Obviously the first thought with vessels and beacons is a lighthouse guiding a ship to shore . . ."

"Obviously," Maggie said sarcastically, shooting Tanya a confused look.

". . . but that doesn't make a whole lot of sense, since we're hours from the coastline, and the river doesn't have any lighthouses. It must be a metaphor for something, but we aren't sure what yet."

"But in *Tales of the Night Queen*, we did find a poem that we think is about the mirror," Kawanna said. She opened up a slim, red volume and slid her finger down to the middle of the page.

Silver quicks and silver dies
To forge a glass where darkness lies
Shatter once and powers fall
But slivers do the Night Queen call
Kissed with crimson drops of rain
They bring the Queen to rise again

"If that is about the mirror," Tanya said, "I really don't like the part about the slivers calling to the queen."

"And what's that line about red rain? Is it like pollution or something?" Maggie asked.

Suddenly, Tanya paled. "Oh, wait. I think I know what it means." She bit her lip and squeezed her hands together in her lap. "The poem says that shattering the mirror broke the queen's power, but the slivers still have a connection with her."

"Well, yeah, that was our theory even before we found the poem, right?" Clio said.

"I'm talking about the other bit. About the crimson drops of rain." Tanya's fingertips ran over the thin scar of the cut she had gotten a few weeks earlier. "I accidentally sliced my finger on one of the mirror pieces, and the dreams started right afterward." She forced herself to meet the eyes of her friends. "I think when I cut myself, I might have opened something up . . . something that will bring the Night Queen back into our world."

CHAPTER
12

THERE WAS A long silence as Tanya's friends took in what she had just told them. "The crimson drops," Clio said. "You think that's the blood from when you cut your finger."

Tanya nodded. "And the next line says that the blood brings the queen to rise again."

"Rise again?" Maggie blanched. "Does that mean she'll, like, come into our world?" Her green eyes widened, and she clutched Tanya's arm. "What if it's already happened? She could be putting together an army of *lusus naturae* right now to come after us!"

"Slow down. If she was already here, we'd definitely know by now, so let's not panic," Rebecca said.

"Easy for you to say! You're not the one who

almost got dragged to her doom by rotting, undead corpse arms!"

"Listen, we don't know for sure that Tanya's right about what the poem means," Clio said. "And there still might be a way to destroy the mirror shards before they can really do anything besides cause bad dreams." Clio's eyes narrowed. "When's the next full moon?"

"Why do we need to know that?" Ethan asked.

"Because whenever anything big goes down, it's *always* on the full moon," Clio answered.

"Ugh. That's true," Maggie agreed. "It's like some kind of Nightmare Realm power source or something."

"Let me check the calendar," Tanya said. She pulled up an app on her phone, and when she spoke again her voice was heavy. "That's next Sunday."

"That gives us just a few days to figure out how to destroy the mirror pieces and stop the queen from rising again." Rebecca looked at her watch and loaded the extra cinnamon rolls back into the Tupperware she had brought. "The library opens in fifteen minutes. I'll keep digging over there to see if there's anything else in the town history records that might help us. Maggie, can you come with me and help?"

"Do I have to?" Maggie rolled her eyes. Seeing

Rebecca's folded arms, she sighed. "Ugh. Fine. But I won't like it."

"I do love making you suffer," Rebecca teased. "Clio, did you and Kawanna find any connection between the mirror and the doll? Anything about why the mirror would make Tanya have dreams about Mary Rose? There has to be a link. If Tanya's blood on the mirror is what woke up Mary Rose, then maybe neutralizing the mirror will deactivate Mary Rose, too."

Clio and Kawanna looked at each other. "We'll keep searching," Kawanna said.

Clio put her hand on Tanya's shoulder. "Don't worry, though, my auntie can work solo later so I can still come with you when you babysit."

"We don't have time to worry about that right now," Tanya said, ignoring the anxious roiling in her stomach. "Mary Rose is definitely trouble, but she's not as dangerous as the mirror could be." She stood up straighter and forced a smile. "I'm sure I can handle her on my own. The shards are the key. I think you should stay here with your aunt."

Ethan gathered up the plates and stacked them neatly on the counter. "I'll help you, too, Clio. Tanya, do you still have that book I lent you? I think I remember something in there about getting rid of haunted objects."

"Oh, yeah. I forgot to give it back to you. It's in my bag," Tanya reached into her backpack and handed the book over to Ethan. "But the Nightmare Realm is totally different from the Spirit Realm. Do you really think something that works for ghosts would also work for the Night Queen?"

Ethan shrugged. "I guess there's only one way to find out."

. . . . .

Later that afternoon, Tanya's feet dragged along the sidewalk as she approached the Fogelman house. It was the absolute last place she wanted to be, especially by herself. But Tanya knew her friends were working together to take care of the mirror shards, and that had to be the priority. If the shards really could cause the Night Queen to rise again at the next full moon, the girls were already cutting it close enough as it was; that gave them only a few days to find a solution before it was too late. She only wished she could be there helping instead of heading into another night with Mary Rose.

As she walked up the steps, Tanya gave herself a pep talk, running Rebecca's reassuring words back through her mind. Whatever Mary Rose's power was, it couldn't be very strong. She might be some kind of possessed doll, but all she really seemed to want to do was hang out with Kira. And what could one doll really do anyway? Tanya was bigger and stronger. If the doll tried anything, Tanya was sure she could stop it if she had to. *But it won't try anything. Not as long as I don't let it know that I know.* It was a strange thought, but she sensed in her gut that it was true. As long as Mary Rose believed that Tanya thought she was an ordinary doll, then Mary Rose would have to act like an ordinary doll.

When Tanya walked inside the house, she already knew without asking that Kira would be upstairs in the doll room. Mrs. Fogelman disappeared out the back door to her studio, and Tanya made her way slowly up the staircase and down the hall. She tapped on the door of the doll room, and when Kira didn't answer, Tanya pushed it open.

At first, Tanya couldn't see Kira at all, but then she found her. The little girl was curled up on the daybed, whispering to Mary Rose and the dozens of other dolls she had piled on the bed around her. Kira's narrow face was more pinched than usual, and there were dark hollows under her eyes. Her skin had a slightly gray cast, and her thin lips were pale.

In contrast, Mary Rose looked more alive than ever. The doll's marble-white skin had a dewy glow, and its cheeks and lips were as pink and fresh as the first summer roses. The painted blue eyes sparkled, and the gleaming ringlets glowed like sunshine. Kira had dressed the doll in a new dress, ivory white with an embroidered bodice and a lapis cameo brooch pinned at its throat.

"Hi, Kira," Tanya said cautiously. "Mary Rose looks pretty fancy today. Did you get her a new dress?"

"Auntie Dot found that," Kira answered. She pointed to a small upright trunk open on the floor like a doll-sized closet. A row of long dresses hung on tiny hangers on one side of the trunk, and the other held a small mirror and a few cardboard drawers covered in floral-patterned fabric. Tanya remembered seeing something similar in Maggie's room.

"That's cool." Tanya knelt down and took one of the hangers off the little rack inside the trunk. On it hung a forest-green taffeta dress with puffy sleeves and a wide lace collar. It reminded Tanya of the picture she had seen of Elee in the old newspaper clipping. "These look handmade. I bet it would take forever to sew something like this."

"Auntie Dot said that every girl who had Mary Rose learned to sew so they could make her clothes. She says she might teach me to sew, too." Kira sounded sleepy and wan, but Tanya could hear the hope in the little girl's voice. If Mrs. Fogelman would only finish her sculpture, maybe she and Kira would be able to keep each other company instead of rattling around the house like two marbles in an empty can.

"That sounds like fun. I wish I knew how to sew." She put the dress back and pulled out another. This one was a rich, plum velvet with a bustle in the back. "I bet this would look really pretty on Mary Rose. Do you want to bring her over here and we can play with her together?" The idea of touching Mary Rose—or even being near her—was almost unbearable, but it was far worse to imagine what the doll might do if it was out of her sight.

"Why?" Kira asked suspiciously. "You never wanted to play with her before."

"I don't know," Tanya said. "You just seem to have a lot of fun with her, so I thought I'd try to play, too." She worked to keep her face bland and her voice natural, like she hadn't really thought about it much. She wondered if Mary Rose was listening, and Tanya tried not to let her eyes slide over to stare at the doll.

"I guess so," Kira said sluggishly. She slithered out from between the dolls piled on the daybed and dragged herself over to sit on the floor beside Tanya. Kira's eyes were dull, and she moved mechanically as she tugged the new dress onto Mary Rose.

Tanya opened the little drawers in the trunk and

found a pair of kid boots with tiny black pearl buttons. "Here. Do you want to put these on her?" Kira took them without looking at them and slipped them onto the doll's feet. Tanya tried to smile. "She looks great. Where do you think she's going in such a fancy dress?"

"I don't know," Kira said.

"Well, where do you want to pretend she's going?" Tanya asked.

"Nowhere," Kira said. Tanya felt like she was floundering. Wasn't this what little kids did when they played with dolls? They dressed them up and pretended things? She wished Maggie were with her; Maggie would know exactly what to do.

"Well, then what do you want to do with Mary Rose instead? How do you like to play with her?" Tanya had always preferred more practical ways to spend her time, like building things and taking them apart. Maybe kids who liked dolls had some other kinds of games that Tanya didn't know about.

Kira set the doll on the floor. "It's boring to play dolls when you're here. Mary Rose is my forever best friend, and we like to be alone."

"Okay," Tanya said, wondering if Kira had seen Mary Rose move or if the doll had talked to her, but knowing that she couldn't ask. "Why don't you bring

Mary Rose downstairs with us, and she can watch us set up the science experiment I brought?"

Kira stood up and carried the doll over to the day-bed. "I want to leave her up here."

"No!" Tanya interjected, too quickly. Kira froze, and her eyes narrowed. The air seemed to go out of the room, and it was not just Kira and Mary Rose that Tanya felt watching her. It was all the dolls. Tanya knew the other dolls weren't like Mary Rose; they were no different than the ones she had grown up with or seen at friends' houses, but suddenly she could swear she felt their gaze, cold and calculating like the flat black eyes of sharks in an aquarium. "It's just that, well, last time I was here you wanted to bring her everywhere, and I thought maybe you'd like to have her with you this time, too. But it's fine. You can leave her up here if you want." The air came back into the room then, and the other dolls' eyes lost that watchful look, returning instead to the vague half smiles, guileless and blank once again.

Downstairs in the kitchen, Tanya tried to coax Kira into eating dinner, but the little girl just picked at her food, nibbling at the edges and pushing the rest around her plate. Kira's eyelids were heavy, and Tanya decided to forget about the science project she had planned. "Do you want to read a book together instead, or maybe watch something on your iPad?" Tanya asked. She put a hand on Kira's forehead, but her skin was cool and dry. "Are you feeling okay?"

Kira yawned. "I'm sleepy. Can I go to bed?"

"I guess," Tanya said, surprised. It wasn't even seven o'clock yet. "But are you sure you're not sick? Do you want me to go get your auntie Dot from her studio?"

"I'm not sick," Kira insisted. "I didn't sleep that much last night. My mom says that it's important to get lots of sleep."

Tanya felt a pang of sympathy. The little girl must have talked to her mother earlier, and she was probably feeling homesick. That would explain why she was so listless and droopy. Tanya held out her hand. "Come on. I'll take you upstairs." Kira allowed herself to be led without protest, her feet scuffing up the steps.

A short while later, Kira's eyes were already closing by the time Tanya had closed the bedroom door, smiling to herself. Kira had allowed herself to be tucked in, and she had even agreed to listen to a few pages of the book, *Wicked Bugs*, that Tanya had brought to read.

For a moment, Tanya allowed herself to luxuriate

in the feeling that this was just an ordinary baby-sitting job. It was nice to have a break from Mary Rose for a while, and Tanya was relieved that Kira hadn't asked to bring the doll to bed with her. But then she wondered if it was only because Kira knew that soon enough the little kid boots would make their creeping way down the hall to keep her company.

And now that Kira was asleep, and Mrs. Fogelman was still in her studio for another hour or two, Tanya was loath to realize that she was alone with Mary Rose. She stood in the hallway, unsure of what to do. She hated the idea of spending a single extra second upstairs in the doll room, but it was just as unnerving to imagine sitting downstairs and hearing tiny footsteps patter overhead like a rat scuttling in the rafters. Tanya finally decided to bring the doll back downstairs with her. Mary Rose seemed less frightening when she was away from the other dolls, and it would keep her away from Kira, too.

Before she could lose her nerve, Tanya pushed open the door to the doll room and flicked on the light. Something in the room's air felt different, the way it might feel to stumble into the middle of a private conversation. There were still piles of dolls seated in clusters around the bed, but had some of them moved? The one with the yarn hair had its hands folded neatly at its waist. Hadn't one arm been flung out across the pillow before? And the bride doll with the ruffled full skirt. Tanya could swear she remembered the veil had been covering the doll's face, but now it was lifted back behind its hair.

And there at the center of them was Mary Rose. Tanya didn't allow herself to wonder if Mary Rose had moved; she didn't allow herself to look at all, afraid that her face would betray what she knew and believed about the doll, and all pretense would vanish. She thought of the dream again, and the way that the doll had turned its head, looked right into Tanya's eyes, and winked. Tanya could not face that in real life, not yet, anyway, so without looking, she walked quickly over to the bed, murmuring something about how much she bet Mrs. Fogelman would want to see that Kira had been trying the new dresses on her doll. Tanya said it like she was talking to herself, like this wasn't a performance she was putting on for the benefit of all the dolls in the room. Dolls that should be ordinary things, just parts of a room to be played with or forgotten or discarded, like a block or a board game or an empty glass. And not this other thing that breathed and crouched expectantly just at the edge of her vision.

Last year at one of the girls' Friday Films, they had

watched an old horror movie called *The Birds*. Tanya and her friends had laughed at how corny the special effects were, but what she remembered most was a scene when the main characters were walking from the car to the house, and they noticed hundreds of birds—thousands of them, even—perched on every branch and streetlight and roof, watching them. Watching and waiting. This is what it felt like when Tanya leaned forward, clasped her hands around Mary Rose's waist, and picked her up.

She did not flinch when her fingers closed around the lumpy softness of the doll's middle, or when the cold porcelain arm brushed against her hand. Somehow, she felt sure that if she did, the careful, taut edges of the room would collapse like an imploding star, and Tanya would be crushed beneath the weight of the dolls as they descended upon her and crawled over her like lice.

Easy, girl, Tanya thought to herself. Mary Rose's insides seemed to squirm beneath her fingers like worms, and Tanya almost dropped her. She tried to remember her first chemistry set, how carefully she had learned to handle the delicate glass beakers as she carried them over to her desk. *You've carried hydrochloric acid*, she told herself. *You can carry this*. To calm herself, Tanya ran the periodic table through her mind, combining elements and reciting the formula of each compound she knew by heart. *Water: H_2O. Salt: NaCl. Carbon Dioxide: CO_2.*

Tanya wanted to rush down the stairs as soon as possible, but she forced herself to take her time, popping her head into Kira's room to check on the sleeping girl, turning out the upstairs lights as she went. Mary Rose hung limply in her hand, and her head lolled to one side when Tanya propped her in a chair and smoothed down the velvet skirt. "There," Tanya said aloud. "Mrs. Fogelman will love that."

Tanya's phone buzzed, and she pulled it out of her pocket.

[Clio 7:06 PM] How's it going?

[Tanya 7:07 PM] OK I guess . . . ?

[Clio 7:07 PM] Anything weird?

[Tanya 7:07 PM] Nothing weirder than usual
How about over there?

[Clio 7:09 PM] Ethan found something for the mirror. We think it will work

[Tanya 7:10 PM] You THINK it will? What if it doesn't?

[Maggie 7:13 PM] ITS GOING TO WORK!!!

[Rebecca 7:13 PM] *It's*

[Maggie 7:13 PM] STOP IT

[Tanya 7:13 PM] When? Are u doing it tonight?

[Rebecca 7:13 PM] Tomorrow

[Ethan 7:13 PM] We think it will work better if ur there

[Tanya 7:14 PM] OK. I hope it works

[Maggie 7:14 PM] DONT WORRY IT WILL!!!!!

[Rebecca 7:14 PM] *don't*

Tanya grinned. Her friends always knew just the right thing to say. Everything was going to be okay. It had to be. She yawned and stretched, feeling her wrists crack as her arms extended overhead. She snuck a glance at Mary Rose. Still in the chair, just as Tanya had left her.

Not quite.

The doll had slipped down the seat so that its legs were dangling off the edge. Its arms were splayed out at its sides, and its chin slumped against its neck. Its mouth had the hint of a smirk, as if daring Tanya to react. What kind of game was this? Tanya stood up and pushed Mary Rose back into place and positioned the doll's hands carefully in its lap. She looked at her watch. Just one more hour until Mrs. Fogelman returned.

Tanya had to go to the bathroom. She stood up, but then she hesitated. Should she bring Mary Rose with her? She snuck a glance at the doll. It would be way too weird to start carrying it from room to room all of a sudden. Maybe Tanya could just wait for Mrs. Fogelman. She looked at her watch again. There was no way she could hold it that long. She would have to go and leave Mary Rose unattended in the living room.

Tanya walked casually out of the room, but as soon as she turned the corner, she raced down the hall to the bathroom. She locked the door behind her and hurried through her business, her hands trembling as she washed them in the sink. Her heart hammered in her chest when she returned to the living room and found Mary Rose's chair empty.

Tanya caught a flash of movement at the edge of her vision. She whirled around, but it was just a neighbor's car lights reflecting off a glass-covered print on the wall. Tanya heard a titter, and she spun again, trying to locate the sound. Was it coming from the kitchen? She ran to the source of the sound, all pretense gone now. The kitchen was still, but there was an egg broken on the floor in front of the refrigerator, and Tanya let out a cry of horror.

She heard another giggle and the scuttle of little feet on the steps. Tanya ran back to the hall. A tiny kid shoe sat on the staircase, the black pearl button gleaming dully under the overhead light. *Kira's room*, Tanya thought. But as she arrived at Kira's door, she heard a giggle farther down the hall, and then a door slammed, making her jump. Mary Rose had gone back to the doll room.

Tanya felt sick. Her stomach was twisted in knots, and her breath was short and tight. She pushed open Kira's door to find the little girl alone and sleeping soundly. Tanya closed the door behind her and stood at the top of the stairs, staring back at the doll-room door. What would she see if she opened it now?

Tanya heard Mrs. Fogelman coming through the back door. "Yoo-hoo," the artist called from below. "I'm back!" Tanya's body felt wooden as she walked downstairs and into the kitchen. She quietly packed her things as Mrs. Fogelman chattered away at her about the sculpture. "I just put on the finishing touches tonight. I can't wait to mount it in its proper spot of honor in the yard!"

But all Tanya could think about was Mary Rose. She felt sick at the thought of leaving Kira at the doll's mercy, but she didn't have a choice. It was almost like the doll had been tormenting Tanya, intentionally frightening her and taunting her into revealing her suspicions. And whatever game Mary Rose was playing, Tanya was sure it would only get worse.

CHAPTER
13

EARLY THE NEXT morning, Tanya stood with her friends in a park just a short walk from Kawanna's downtown shop. It was a cold, raw day, and they were the only ones in the soggy little patch that ran along the river's edge. The landscape here was bleak in winter, and their bright coats were the only spots of color to be seen.

The sun was only just beginning to rise, and mist still sat heavy on the river. Tanya had her gray knit beanie pulled down tightly over her ears, and her striped scarf was looped as high as it would go around her neck. Her hands were growing numb inside her fingerless gloves, and she shoved them deep into the pockets of her coat to warm up. Maggie yawned next to her and pulled the neck of her fuzzy pink jacket up over her face. "Ugh. Tell me again why we have to do this so early?"

Ethan squatted down next to the hole he and Clio had dug at the roots of a large shrub. "For the mist."

"Oh, of course. Right. For the mist." Maggie rolled her eyes. "Do you have any idea what he's talking about?" she mumbled to Tanya.

"Nope," Tanya answered. "But I was babysitting the possessed doll last night, remember? You were the ones who were supposed to be making the plan. Are you telling me you don't even remember what the plan *is*?"

"I don't know, it was based on some poem or something," Maggie said. "And part of it was an annoying riddle, which Clio obviously figured out in, like, five seconds, so after that I got kind of bored."

"I'll show you," Rebecca said. "We wrote everything down in here so you would have it for your research." She pulled Tanya's notebook out of her backpack and opened it to a page where she had written down a few lines of verse next to a hand-drawn map. "Since you couldn't be there last night I took the best notes I could. I tried to make them really neat and easy to read."

"Thanks," Tanya said. She looked down at the poem Rebecca had copied into her book.

Dipped in summer's golden glow
Trapped in mist where waters flow
Buried 'neath the rowan tree
Blood undone, returned to thee

"I see where the mist comes in, but what's 'summer's golden glow'?" Tanya asked.

"We're pretty sure it's honey," Clio answered. She walked over and pointed to a little doodle of a bee that Rebecca had drawn near the poem. "There was a little pen-and-ink drawing of a bee hidden in the artwork next to the poem Ethan found. I had Rebecca copy it into your notebook, too."

"It makes sense," Tanya said thoughtfully. "Bees make honey in summer. It's gold, and you can dip things in it."

"You would say that," Maggie said. "Nobody ever likes *my* ideas."

"What did you think summer's golden glow would be?" Tanya asked.

"I don't know, like a sunlamp or something."

"A *sunlamp*?" Tanya asked. "You do know they hadn't been invented yet when this poem was written, right?"

"Well, duh. I figured it meant the actual summer sun, but since it's winter and we couldn't get that, I was *improvising*," Maggie said. "It's something actors do. You wouldn't understand."

Tanya grinned. "You're right about that." She pulled the bag of mirror shards out of a brown paper envelope, careful not to cut herself again on the sharp edges. "Where should we put these?"

"I'll take them," Rebecca said. She squatted over a chipped china bowl and filled it with honey from a jar. She upended the bag into the bowl and watched as the silver slivers settled themselves along the surface and slowly sank. She poked them down with a stick until they were all covered. "There we go. Dipped in summer's golden glow. Step one is complete."

Tanya read the next line of the poem and grinned when she saw Clio unscrew a large mason jar. Using a wooden spoon, Tanya helped pour the honey and mirror pieces into the jar. "Now I see how we're going to trap the mist," she said.

Clio waded into the river, careful to keep the water level below the tops of her Union Jack Wellingtons, and swooped the jar through the mist around her. She clapped the lid back down and screwed it on tightly. She came back to the group and held up the jar. The mist was already condensing into beads of water along the sides. "Trapped that flowing water mist like a champ," she said. "Step two is done." She fist-bumped Ethan and put the jar on the ground.

"Next we just need to bury it here," Ethan said, pointing to the hole they had dug. "This is a rowan tree. Locally we call them mountain ash, but rowan trees have a long link with magic and mythology. In the UK, they believed the rowan protected against witchcraft, and the Vikings used its wood to make their rune staves, which were kind of like talismans."

"Now do you see why I got kinda bored last night?" Maggie said into Tanya's ear.

"I heard that," Clio said.

"I know," Maggie said, her eyes sparkling impishly. "Let's pick up the pace, Ethan. Some of us have shows to binge-watch later."

"Take your time, Ethan," Tanya said. "We really need this to work."

"It's gonna work," Maggie answered. "It always does. Seriously. When has one of these things ever *not* worked?"

"Be careful what you say," Rebecca chastised. "There's a first time for everything, and we don't want this to be our first screw-up."

Ethan nestled the jar in the hole between the tree's roots, and the five of them filled the cavity with dirt. "Now what?" Tanya looked up from the notes she was scribbling in her notebook. "How will we know we're successful? Do we need to come back and check on it?"

"We should know right away," Ethan said. "Watch this." He unburied the jar and held it up, squinting. Tanya gasped. Collected in the condensation on the sides were three droplets of blood. "May I return your blood to you, madam?" he asked in a goofy voice.

Maggie snickered, and Ethan blushed and shot a quick glance at Clio before looking away again.

Tanya pulled off her gloves and carefully unscrewed the jar lid. The three drops trembled onto her finger and disappeared. "That is unbelievable," she whispered. "I would give anything to understand the science behind this." She screwed the jar shut again. She jotted a few things down in her notebook, her mind already working through possible explanations.

"I know you're hoping we'll let you keep that jar to study, but we just can't risk it. Putting it back under the tree roots seems like the safest idea," Clio said. "If rowan trees offer protection against magic, then I can't think of a better place to keep those mirror bits out of harm's way." They reburied the jar, and Rebecca passed out wipes to clean their hands.

Tanya was surprised at how much lighter she felt. She took a deep breath and relaxed her shoulders.

"Feel better?" Clio asked.

Tanya nodded. "It's amazing how accidentally almost bringing an undead queen back to take over the earth can really stress a person out."

Clio laughed. "You think?" She and the others gathered up their things and headed back to the park entrance.

"Is this the part where we go out for waffles?" Maggie asked. "I was promised waffles."

"A waffle break is definitely in order," Rebecca said. "But then we have to get back to work. There's still the doll to deal with."

"But if Tanya's blood on the mirror really is what activated Mary Rose, then didn't we just deactivate her?" Maggie asked.

"I hope so," Tanya said. But she wished there was some kind of controlled experiment they could do to know for sure. *Hey, not every hypothesis can be perfectly tested*, she told herself. *Even gravity is just a theory*. Maybe a theory would be enough this time. What a relief it would be not to spend every waking moment worrying about Kira and Mary Rose, and the way Kira grew frailer and weaker as the doll seemed to grow more powerful.

Rebecca shook her head. "Hoping isn't enough. We need to find a way to be sure we shut her down for good. And that's gonna take a lot more research."

Maggie groaned. "*More* research? Way to make me lose my appetite, Becks!"

Rebecca put her arm around her friend's shoulder. "Poor baby! Don't worry. If you lost your appetite, we can totally skip the waffles."

"Don't you dare!" Maggie cried.

"Uh-huh. That's what I thought," Rebecca teased, and Maggie laughed along with the others. The sun peeped through a break in the clouds, making the dew on the grass glitter like tiny gems. Hope soared in Tanya's heart. With her friends by her side, she was sure that stopping Mary Rose would be a piece of cake.

CHAPTER 14

A FEW HOURS later, Tanya looked up from the mound of books and the open laptop in front of her. Her eyes were dry and sandy, and her back and neck ached from hunching over for so long. But she felt the same thrill she felt after conducting a difficult experiment. It was the thrill of discovery. "I think I found something."

Clio looked up from her beanbag chair. "Is it about the doll?"

"No, but it answers another question I've been wondering about," Tanya answered. "It's related to alchemy."

"Say what, now?" Maggie asked.

Tanya held up a dark brown book titled *Alchemy and the Art of Crossing Realms*. "Alchemy was this false belief that with the right chemicals, people could turn other metals into gold. It was scientifically debunked, obviously, since gold is an element, and you can't make elements out of other elements. Well, unless we're talking about radioactive half-lives or something . . ."

"Already bored. Get to the point," Maggie said.

"Sorry. Anyway, not every person interested in alchemy was trying to make gold. The word originated in ancient Egypt, and its earliest followers were interested not in gold, but in immortality."

"Still bored," Maggie said.

"Ugh. Fine. Basically, some alchemists believed that the right combination of chemical elements could give them special powers. Like the ability to travel to other realms."

Ethan perked up from his spot in the corner. "The spirit hole!"

"That's right," Tanya said. "Remember what you said to me? 'Iron closes, but gold opens.' Basically, different chemical elements have different properties and powers. I *knew* there had to be some connection between science and the supernatural."

"Yay for you," Maggie said. "But how does this help us stop the Night Queen?"

"Well, one of the things that's been bothering

me is that the Night Queen has power over certain objects, right? And then there's other stuff that she doesn't. Like why could she control this *one* mirror, but not any other mirror? *One* clock, but not all the clocks?"

"That's easy," Maggie said. "Because a bunch of weirdos made stuff like the mirror and the clock especially for her. They, like, waved their hands over it or added a unicorn hair or whatever, and then *Boom!* It belonged to the Night Queen."

"I always suspected there must be some kind of chemical reason for it. Something the objects have in common." Tanya grinned. "And I think I found it." She held up the book. A woodcut illustration showed a muscular man with a toga and curly hair. He wore winged sandals. Next to him was an old man with a long beard hunched over a bubbling cauldron. Smoke from the cauldron curled up into the sky, where a face was framed in rays like the sun.

"That's Hermes," Clio said, pointing to the man in the toga. "The messenger of the gods."

"It is," Tanya said. "And what's his Roman name?"

"Mercury!" Clio cried. "The first line of the poem: 'Silver quicks and silver dies.' *Quicksilver* is another name for *mercury*."

Tanya nodded. "Diamond dust mirrors were

made using mercury. And guess what else had mercury in them? The pendulums in old clocks. I think that the mercury must work as a kind of conductor. It can't open or close a portal or anything like that, but it can allow the Night Queen to control whatever has the mercury in it. Sort of like how a hacker can take over your computer and use it to do stuff or spy on you."

Maggie cocked her head and thought a moment. "I can't believe I'm saying this, but I think I actually get it." Her mouth quirked. "But what does that have to do with the doll?"

Tanya sighed. "Nothing." She closed the book and pushed it aside. "But I was happy just to find *something*, even if it's not actually useful."

Rebecca pushed her bangs out of her eyes. "Hey, that's totally useful. Knowing what has mercury in it could help us figure out where the Night Queen might strike next. We may have stopped her this time with the mirror shards, but that doesn't mean she won't try again."

"Yeah, but that still doesn't explain Mary Rose," Tanya said. "It's not like people run around putting mercury in dolls. That stuff is seriously poisonous. So if Mary Rose isn't some Night Queen minion, then what *is* she?" She threw up her hands in frustration. "Why can't we *find* anything?"

Ethan's eyes widened behind his glasses. "Maybe we're just looking in the wrong place." He bent down and frantically started leafing through a book. "Clio, what was that stuff you and Kawanna found the other day about vessels and beacons? Do you remember what it said?"

Clio and Kawanna sorted through the stacks of rumpled journals and yellowed papers spread out on the counter. "Here it is," Kawanna finally said. She held up a dog-eared old notebook with a stained black cover and turned to a page near the end. Over her shoulder, Tanya could just make out Miss Pearl's jagged, spidery handwriting in ink that had faded to sepia brown. Tanya held up the book and started reading: *"The beacon calls to her in the light of the moon, and the vessel carries her back. Without the beacon, the vessel is rudderless, a hollow husk doomed to wait and wander. But the beacon guides the vessel's heart. And once she returns, she will rule both realms with fists of blood and silver."*

"Ooo-kaaay," Maggie said. "That sounds like something I would say when I had a high fever."

"We've been looking for something about a doll, right?" Ethan said. "Maybe we haven't found anything because Mary Rose wasn't made to be a doll."

"What do you mean?" Rebecca asked. "What was she made to be?"

Ethan held up the green *Object Possession* book in his hand. "In this book, the haunted objects weren't just spooky stuff that went flying around the room. They were kind of like homes for the spirits that lived in them. They were *vessels*." He flipped through the pages until he found an ink drawing of a ship at sea, manned by ghosts. "This is a drawing of the *Flying Dutchman*, a ghost ship supposedly sailed by an entire crew of spirits." He put the book down. "What if Mary Rose is like that? What if *she's* the vessel?"

"A vessel for *what*?" Rebecca asked.

"The Night Queen," Ethan answered. "What if Mary Rose was built as a means to bring the Night Queen back? Maybe there was a way that the queen's spirit could possess the doll, and then once this beacon thing turns on or whatever, she can come back for real and take over."

Tanya looked at the words in the journal again. "So let's say Ethan's right." She pulled out her notebook and a pencil and started jotting down her thoughts as she spoke. "If the Night Queen has possessed Mary Rose, then it means she's looking for a way to come back for real, in her true form. But to do that, she needs at least two things: moonlight—which obviously means the full moon—and whatever this beacon is. As long as we destroy the beacon, then the Night Queen still has no way to come back."

Maggie sighed. "I'm so tired of finding and destroying things. Aren't we done with all that?"

"I don't know," Rebecca said. "But I think we might be." She flipped to a page in the red *Tales of the Night Queen* book. There was a detailed drawing of a bubble-like sphere with a grandfather clock and a gilded frame mirror inside of it; lines like rays of light surrounded the picture. The Night Queen's face was faintly visible in the background. "I think maybe the mirror and the clock *were* the beacons."

"And both of those *were* already destroyed, right?" Tanya asked excitedly. "Are you telling me we already beat her?"

"Pretty much," Rebecca answered. "But I don't think the Night Queen knows that yet."

"So instead of trying to stop the Night Queen at her most powerful, all we have to do is deal with one eensy-weensy doll?" Maggie asked. "That's easy! We can just tie it in a bag and throw it in the river or something."

Tanya toyed with her pencil. "Actually, it's not that easy. Kira's going through a hard time, and she's gotten really attached to Mary Rose. Plus the doll has been a treasured family heirloom for, like, a hundred years. Both Kira and Mrs. Fogelman would be devastated if we just got rid of it." She doodled in the margins of her notebook. "I think we have to find a way to make sure we deactivate Mary Rose and turn her back into a normal doll. For good."

"But she's not a normal doll!" Maggie protested. "She's *evil*! You said so yourself!" She turned to Rebecca and Ethan. "And what about the guy who made her? He was a total creeper with a grudge against the family! You know he put all kinds of nasty stuff in there."

Tanya shook her head firmly. "I don't care. I'm not destroying a little girl's favorite doll. It would be like taking away her best friend." She folded her arms across her chest.

"I can't believe this!" Maggie cried. "If we get rid of the doll, then we get rid of the Night Queen's last chance to come into our world. We can save the day! Forever! And you won't do it?" She looked around at the others to gather support, but no one spoke. "Come on, guys. Be real for a second. None of you really thinks we can finally defeat the Night Queen without destroying Mary Rose, do you?"

Tanya was resolute. "Then we just have to find another way."

CHAPTER 15

TANYA LAY IN bed the next morning looking over the list she had started.

WAYS TO UN-POSSESS MARY ROSE:

- Smoke from burning sage?
- Holy water?
- Feed her something besides blood? Milk? Angel food cake?

She tore the list out of her notebook and crumpled it up in frustration. None of these had any scientific basis, and some of them were simply ideas from old movies Maggie had made her watch. The beacons had already been destroyed anyway. Maybe Mary Rose really was just a normal doll again. Maybe they were just worrying over nothing.

Tanya thought again of the words Kawanna had read from the old journal: *Without the beacon, the vessel is rudderless, a hollow husk doomed to wait and wander.* They had to make sure that the Night Queen wasn't still possessing Mary Rose. Otherwise she could be stuck inside the doll forever, growing angrier and angrier. Tanya remembered the broken egg and the nasty little scuttling sounds in Mrs. Fogelman's house. Maybe the queen couldn't take her true form and come back to earth anymore, but that didn't mean she couldn't still cause mischief or hurt someone. Even a doll could get revenge.

Tanya sighed. Maybe Maggie was right. Maybe they should just destroy Mary Rose and pretend it was an accident. But then Tanya thought about Kira, so lonely and homesick, and how much she relied on the doll. If only Mrs. Fogelman would finish her creepy sculpture and focus on helping Kira when the little girl needed her most! Of course it wasn't that simple, though, and Tanya knew it. She may not understand much about the reasons why adults did things, but she was pretty sure the sculpture was Mrs. Fogelman's way of dealing with losing Eli.

Tanya flopped back on her pillow and stared at the

ceiling. It was all just so sad. And after school, she would be over there again. But at least she wouldn't be alone this time. She reached for her phone and texted Clio.

Everyone still on for babysitting today?

Yes! After school?

Rebecca's bringing the salt
Ethan has a silver box he's lending us
I have the sage

???

Didn't you see the other texts?!?

Tanya quickly switched over to check the text chain between her friends and Kawanna. Ethan had sent a screenshot of a torn page, yellowed and crumpled. The words *Freeing the Vessel* were written in elegant script at the top of the page. Tanya felt a grin begin to spread as she read through the exchange. They had found it! A way to make Mary Rose a normal doll without destroying her. And it was easy! The only hard part would be to convince Kira to give up Mary Rose for a little while, but Tanya was sure they could figure out something. Finally, things were looking up.

. . . . .

Mrs. Fogelman seemed different when she let the four girls into her house. She had bags under her eyes, and her curls hung limply around her face. Her lips were bare, and her olive skin looked chalky. Even her clothing was subdued, and Tanya noticed the usual cloud of sandalwood perfume was absent. Tanya introduced her friends and then waited for the artist to make her typical beeline for the studio. But instead, Mrs. Fogelman gestured to the living room sofa, inviting them to take a seat. She sank down into a green-striped armchair across from them. "I'm glad you're all here."

"Thanks." Tanya perched nervously on the chair, waiting for Mrs. Fogelman to say something. When she didn't, Tanya finally ventured a question. "So," she said, "what's up?"

"I finished my sculpture," Mrs. Fogelman answered. "And it is truly a masterpiece."

"Wow," Tanya said. "That's great. How do you feel?"

Mrs. Fogelman rubbed her face in her hands. "Wrung out," she said at last. "Spent. I am but an empty husk of a woman."

"Oh," Tanya said. She snuck a furtive look at the others, who were just as nonplussed as she was.

"Such is the nature of the work," Mrs. Fogelman intoned. "But I must admit I'm a bit more enervated than usual. I always give myself over to my work, but this piece seemed to drain a part of my soul." She swept her hair out of her face and knotted it loosely on top of her head. Her cheekbones looked sharp and angular, and her eyes had a feverish cast. "I'll be spending the rest of the day at a yoga retreat. I should be home no later than seven."

"Got it," Tanya said. "I hope it's really . . . restorative." She folded her hands in her lap. Why were they sitting here? "Well, I guess if there isn't anything else, we should probably go find Kira." Tanya stood up.

"Well, there is just one more thing," Mrs. Fogelman said. Tanya sat back down. "It's about Kira." Tanya felt her shoulders tighten. "She hasn't been herself the last few days. Very listless and sleepy, and she's looking a bit . . . peaked." She shifted in her seat, and Tanya noticed for the first time that the artist's wrists were bare of the Bakelite bracelets she always wore. "I took her to the doctor, but there's nothing physically wrong with her."

"That's a relief," Tanya said.

Mrs. Fogelman ignored her, and her gaze turned to the window and the yard beyond. "She's always been a moody child, but this seems different." She turned back to Tanya, her eyes damp. "I'm worried she's a bit homesick. You know, lonely."

"Sure," Tanya said.

"I was thinking we should do something to cheer her up, don't you agree?"

"That's a great idea," Tanya answered.

"Excellent. I had a marvelous thought as I was putting the finishing touches on my sculpture. It came to me suddenly. Perhaps you girls could have a sleepover here at the house." She picked up a date-book from the side table. "I believe next Monday is a school holiday, so how about Sunday night?"

Tanya looked at the others, who nodded. "Um, we'll have to check with our parents, but that sounds like it could work."

Mrs. Fogelman brushed her hands together. "Well, then. That's settled." She stood up and wavered on her feet for a moment, gripping the back of the chair for support.

"Are you all right?" Clio asked.

"Yes, just a bit light-headed. Not much sleep last night, I'm afraid." She straightened her shoulders and took a deep breath. "There. Much better." She popped her head into the hallway. "Kira, darling! I'm leaving for yoga. Come down and give your auntie Dot a kiss, will you?"

Tanya craned her neck to see the stairwell from her seat on the sofa. Kira padded slowly down the stairs, carrying Mary Rose in one hand. She rubbed her eyes as though she had just been napping. Her dog-print leggings and hot-pink sweater hung on her thin frame. She cuddled against her great-aunt, and Tanya saw a look of genuine affection between them before Kira's eyes slipped back into blankness and she retreated up the stairs again. Frowning, Mrs. Fogelman watched her walk up the stairs for a moment and then turned to the girls again. "I hope you all have a lovely time together." She walked out the front door, closing it behind her.

Once they saw her drive away, Clio pulled a bundle of dried sage out of her bag. "The silver box was too heavy to bring on our bikes, so Aunt Kawanna's going to drive Ethan over with it, along with the salt."

"It's a *lot* of salt," Rebecca said.

"But how are we going to get Mary Rose away from Kira?" Tanya asked.

"That's where I come in," Maggie said. She unzipped her backpack, and bright, sparkly fabrics came tumbling out. "Operation dress-up has commenced! I have a ton of sequined stuff, hot-pink tutus, and just about every hair care product known to man. There's no way Kira can resist this amazingness. I'll head upstairs now and see what she's up to."

"Okay, good," Tanya said. She glanced outside and saw Kawanna's turquoise Scout pulling into the driveway. A few moments later, Ethan heaved a tarnished silver box up the steps, and Kawanna followed behind hauling two canvas shopping bags.

"Where should we set up?" Kawanna asked.

"The backyard," Tanya said. "That way the sage won't set off the smoke detectors."

"Good idea," Rebecca agreed. The girls helped carry the supplies out back to the small patio behind the kitchen. A swirling mosaic pattern wove through the pavement, and Tanya wondered if Mrs. Fogelman had done it herself. Tanya rubbed her arms, thankful that it wasn't raining. It had been unseasonably warm for winter, but it was still cold enough to chill her to the bones. Anemic sunlight filtered through the clouds and onto the pale stalks of the dead plants in the garden. Mrs. Fogelman's sculptures, an odd mix of stone and old junk, were scattered throughout the yard. Tanya couldn't decide if she liked them or not. She noticed the tarp was gone from the former fish pond. In its place was a lumpy mound wrapped in bulky blue blankets. She guessed that must be the new sculpture and was glad it was still covered up. She was in no mood for Mrs. Fogelman's weird, unnerving *Unburied Past*.

Ethan set the silver chest on the pavement and lifted the lid. Every surface, both inside and outside, was intricately patterned. "Wow! It's so beautiful," Tanya said.

"Thanks," Ethan answered. "It was Great-Grandma Moina's."

"Wow," Tanya said. "What did she use it for?"

"Exorcisms, mainly," he answered matter-of-factly. "Rebecca, do you have the salt?"

"Coming right up." Rebecca handed him a heavy blue box of kosher salt and picked up a second one herself. The two of them emptied the boxes of salt into the chest until the bottom was completely covered. Rebecca handed him another box of salt, and they repeated the process.

"This reminds me of the time I visited you in Hollywood, and you took me to that spa in Korea-town," Clio said to Kawanna. "We lay on those salt beds. Do you remember that?"

Her aunt smiled. "Of course I do! Korean spas are one of the few things I really miss about LA." She glanced up at the cold sky. "Well, that and the weather."

"So all we have to do is put the doll in this silver box, cover it in salt, and then wave burning sage over it?" Tanya asked.

"Yep, that's about it," Ethan answered.

"Are you sure there's not something else we have to do?" Tanya asked again.

"Here. See for yourself." Ethan passed her a yellowed sheet of paper. Tanya recognized the page from the text photo.

Tanya read through it again. Ethan was right, but she couldn't help but feel like they were missing something. It just felt way too easy. "Where did you get this?"

Ethan shrugged. "I didn't find it until yesterday. It was folded up and stuck between two pages of that book I lent you, *Object Possession*. It's a lucky thing it popped up when it did."

"Yeah. Lucky," Tanya said. Something about the story made her uneasy.

Kawanna stood up. "I've got to get back to the shop. Everybody all right?"

"We're good," Clio said. "Thanks for your help."

"Yeah, and thanks for the ride, too," Ethan added.

Kawanna winked. "Anything for my favorite niece and her friends."

"Auntie, I'm your *only* niece," Clio shot back.

"Exactly." Kawanna waved and disappeared back into the house.

"I'll go check on Maggie and Kira," Tanya suggested. "Hopefully Maggie's got her distracted enough that we can grab Mary Rose."

"I'll come with you," Rebecca answered. She stood up and dusted off the knees of her camo-print cargo pants, pausing to flick a wet leaf from the toe of her black studded high-tops. As they walked inside, Tanya was relieved to hear Maggie's and Kira's voices floating down from upstairs.

Maggie had managed to get Kira out of the doll room and back into her own room. The two girls stood at the mirror, Maggie chattering on while her chubby fingers deftly wove Kira's lank hair into an elaborate French braid. Kira's eyes still looked dull, but they tracked Maggie's face in the mirror, and Tanya even caught a small smile forming on the little girl's pale lips. *Leave it to Maggie*, Tanya thought. She always knew just the right way to lift someone's spirits.

Tanya introduced Rebecca to Kira. "I like your sneakers," Kira said.

"Thanks," Rebecca answered. She pointed to Kira's

pink unicorn socks. "I like your socks." Kira smiled shyly and looked down at her toes.

"How's it going in here?" Tanya asked.

"Pretty good," Maggie answered. "We're starting with hair, and then we'll move to makeup and costumes before we put on our show."

"A show? That sounds cool," Tanya said. "What are you going to do?"

"Well, I'm obviously going to sing," Maggie said. "What about you, Kira?"

"I'm not sure," Kira answered. "But I'll probably either dance or sing." She yawned. "Maybe I'll just sing. I'm too tired to dance." She pointed over to her bed. "Mary Rose is going to be in the show, too." Tanya's heart sank when she saw the china doll sitting on the bed. She was hoping Kira had left it in the doll room, where they could easily collect it without Kira noticing.

"Sounds great," Tanya said. She shot Maggie a look, and Maggie gave a tiny shrug as if to say, *What was I supposed to do?*

"You know what?" Rebecca said suddenly. "If Mary Rose is going to be in the show, she should get a costume, too." She walked over to the bed and picked up the doll.

Kira's reaction was swift. "What are you doing?!"

she cried. She ran over and snatched the doll out of Rebecca's arms and put it back on the bed. "Don't touch her! She's mine!" She stood in front of the bed and spread her arms wide, blocking Mary Rose from the other girls. High spots of color appeared on both of her cheeks, and the dark circles under her eyes looked hollow. Rebecca looked back at Tanya.

"It's okay, Kira," Tanya said. "We're not taking her forever. We're just helping her get ready for your show, like Maggie's helping you."

"I don't believe you." Kira's lips pulled back, baring her teeth in a feral snarl.

Tanya stood firm. "You can believe me or not, but we're going to take Mary Rose into the other room to get her ready. I'm sorry if that upsets you, but being able to share is part of being a good person."

Tanya leaned over and picked up Mary Rose. Kira screamed like she'd been burned. "Give her back! You're going to ruin her!" She clawed at Tanya's arms, forcing Tanya to hold the doll over her head.

"Kira, stop! I'm trying to hold her carefully, but if you keep attacking me I might drop her." Tanya stepped away from the little girl. She held the doll tightly against her chest, wrapping her arms around it. "Look, Kira. Look. I'm not going to break her. We just need to borrow her for a few minutes." Tanya could feel Mary Rose's cold, porcelain cheek pressing against her collarbone, but the doll's lumpy middle felt strangely hot against her chest, like there was a tiny furnace inside it.

Kira collapsed on the floor in a full-on tantrum, screaming and pounding the carpet with her bony fists. Maggie stood helplessly beside her, freckles stark against her blanched face. Tanya stood in the doorway, torn. She was Kira's babysitter, and it felt wrong to leave her in such a state. She locked eyes with Maggie. "Just go," Maggie said. "I'll stay with Kira."

Tanya and Rebecca ran down the stairs, with Tanya still clutching the doll to her chest. Mary Rose writhed in her arms like a bag of serpents, and Tanya felt a sting against her collarbone. "Ow!"

"What happened?" Rebecca asked.

Tanya gripped Mary Rose tighter and held her up. The doll hung limp and unmoving between her two hands. Its eyes stared vapidly forward, its cold, china face slack and expressionless. But a drop of blood hung from its lips and fell onto the yoke of its dress, staining it red. "I think it bit me." Tanya felt bile rise in her throat. So burying the mirror hadn't stopped Mary Rose at all. Tanya hoped their backup plan would work.

The two girls burst through the back door and ran

over to the salt-filled box on the patio. Tanya pushed Mary Rose down beneath the white grains, and Clio and Ethan poured the rest of the salt over the doll until every scrap was covered. Rebecca slammed the lid shut, and Ethan turned the lock with a little silver key. The box shook violently. Tanya and Rebecca held it down. "Hurry," Tanya said.

With trembling hands, Clio lit the bundle of sage and waved it over the box, thick clouds of fragrant smoke circling the air around their heads, and said:

"Chest of silver, salt, and sage
Free the spirit from its cage
Relinquish now the vessel's helm
Return in glory to your realm."

The struggling in the box slowed, then stopped. Tanya looked around at the others' faces. "Is that it? Did we do it?"

"It seems like it." Ethan swallowed. "What do you think?"

"Uh, yeah. I guess so." Tanya looked down to consult her notebook, and then noticed for the first time that she didn't have it in her hands. It lay open on the ground beside her, the mechanical pencil resting neatly atop a completely blank page. Had they followed all the steps in the right order? Had they forgotten anything? She realized she had no idea.

"Well, the box isn't moving anymore, so that must be a good sign, right?" Clio said. "And we followed all the directions perfectly."

Tanya bit her lip. Had they? Without her notes, how could they know? Ethan went to unlock the chest, and Tanya put her hand on his arm. "Don't open it yet." She picked up her notebook and started writing down everything she could remember, hoping she wasn't leaving anything out. After a few moments, she nodded. "Okay. I think we're good."

Ethan lifted the lid, and Tanya dug through the salt until her hands found Mary Rose. She pulled the doll out and dusted the salt off its hair and dress. Did it look any different? Tanya wasn't sure. Were the cheeks a little less pink, maybe? The eyes a little softer? She palpated the lumpy middle of the doll. It wasn't hot like it had been before, but was it still a little warm? *Well, it would be*, Tanya thought. *Fabric's not a good conductor, so heat loss would hardly be instantaneous.*

Tanya stood up, Mary Rose hanging limply over her arm. "I'll go bring her back to Kira."

Kira still lay on the floor of her room; Maggie sat next to her, softly stroking her hair. "I brought Mary Rose back," Tanya said softly.

Kira lifted her tearstained face from the carpet. "You said you were going to change her outfit for the show, but you didn't." She started to cry again. "You took her for no reason!"

"Well, I thought it might be more fun for us to choose an outfit for her together," Tanya said. She knelt down and held out her hand to Kira. "Should we go to the doll room and pick one out?"

Kira ignored her outstretched hand and instead yanked the doll from Tanya's grasp. "What did you do to her?"

Tanya blinked. "Nothing."

Kira pored over Mary Rose before clutching her close. "You're a liar." Tears squeezed out of the corners of her eyes. "She's different."

"What are you talking about?" Tanya asked. "Look at her. She's exactly the same!"

Kira's voice rose to a scream. "You ruined her! You stole her from me and ruined her, all because you were jealous!" She stood up and pushed Tanya's shoulder, hard. "Get out of my room! I hate you! I hate all of you!"

Tanya and Maggie looked at each other, stunned.

They had managed to save Mary Rose. But had it been worth it?

CHAPTER 16

IT WAS ALREADY dark, and the full moon was obscured by clouds when Tanya and her friends arrived at Mrs. Fogelman's for the sleepover. Kawanna waved to them from the car and gave a thumbs-up before driving away. The mid-winter heat wave was still going strong, and the girls held their jackets in their hands. Rebecca pushed up the sleeves of her navy cashmere sweater. "So, what do you guys think about tonight?"

"I don't know, but I just hope it goes well," Tanya answered. Kira had been sullen and unresponsive for the remainder of their last babysitting visit, and Tanya had been surprised that her great-aunt hadn't called to cancel the slumber party. She had tried to tell Mrs. Fogelman about Kira's tantrum, but the older woman had just waved it away. And now as the girls stood on the porch waiting for someone to answer the door, Tanya wondered if she should have called the day before just to make sure they were still invited.

Mrs. Fogelman was beaming when she opened the door, and Tanya breathed an inward sigh of relief. The artist was obviously still expecting them, and a smile usually meant that Kira was having a good day. "Come on in, girls. Kira is so excited about tonight." Tanya and her friends crowded into the living room and piled their sleeping bags and pillows on the floor.

Kira came barreling down the stairs already dressed in her unicorn nightgown. She still looked pale and thin, but her eyes were brighter. She bounced up and down at the foot of the stairs. "Guess what! Auntie Dot says we can order pizza *and* Chinese food if we want!"

Mrs. Fogelman held up two delivery menus. "That's right, girls, live it up! The world is your oyster!" She put the menus down on the coffee table.

Tanya gestured to the pile of sleeping bags. "Where should we put our things?"

"Kira, dear, where would you like everyone to sleep? There's room here in the living room, or perhaps you'd like everyone in your room instead?"

"The doll room," Kira said.

Tanya blinked. *Seriously, Kira?* She fought a sudden

wave of dizziness. Her smile was tight. "Great!" Her eyes slid over to Maggie, who shrugged one shoulder. *Well, at least Mary Rose can't bite anyone anymore. She's just a regular creepy doll again.*

Mrs. Fogelman drifted toward the kitchen. "I'd like to spend the evening tidying my studio, but I'm here if you need anything, and I'll be back in before you go to bed."

"Sounds good to me," Tanya answered. The girls walked Mrs. Fogelman to the rear door and flicked on the outside lights that lit the walkway to the studio. The backyard sculptures were thrown into stark relief, and Tanya noticed that *Unburied Past* had finally been unwrapped. The area around it still looked mucky, but Tanya could see the pale patch where the fresh cement had been poured to hold it in place. Metal and bits of glass glinted in the weak light cast by the lamps that lined the ground along the path. Mrs. Fogelman gave one final wave before closing the bright blue door, and a moment later, the little square window beside it glowed bright yellow.

Clio held up the two menus. "Okay, everybody, who wants what?"

· · · · ·

A few hours later, all the girls had changed into their pajamas, and the leftover food was put neatly away in the fridge. A board game was still spread out on the coffee table, and slips of paper from their epic charades tournament were crumpled in a bowl in the middle of the floor.

Kira yawned, and Rebecca looked at her watch. "It's getting late. Should we head upstairs and set up our sleeping bags?"

Clio picked up her pillow. "Sounds like a plan to me."

The others grabbed their stuff, but Tanya stayed on the floor. "You guys go ahead. I'm just gonna finish cleaning down here first."

Kira led Rebecca and Clio upstairs, but Maggie hung back. "Are you okay?"

"Yeah, I'm fine." Tanya put the last of the plastic game pieces into the box and slid it back onto the shelf.

"Are you sure?" Maggie asked. "If it helps, I totally know that Mary Rose is just a normal doll now, but I'm still a little scared about sleeping in there." She held her pillow over her head like a weapon. "But don't worry. We can protect each other."

Tanya laughed weakly and picked up the bowl of charades clues. "I just have to dump these and then I'll be up. Save me a spot on the floor near the doorway, just in case."

"You got it." Maggie grabbed Tanya's olive-green sleeping bag and flitted out the door, her fuzzy pink slippers skating across the hardwood floor.

A few moments later, Tanya threw her canvas backpack over her shoulder and scooped up her flannel-cased pillow. Something from her backpack dug into her back and she shifted it, feeling the familiar spine of her notebook. She still carried it everywhere, but she hadn't looked at it for days, not since she had forgotten to record their doll exorcism. To tell the truth, she hadn't been feeling much like a scientist, lately. Science hadn't helped her feel brave around Mary Rose or figure out how to fix any of her supernatural problems. Even so, she felt scattered without her notebook, like there was a piece of her missing, the piece that kept her grounded and focused.

As Tanya reached the top of the stairs, she heard the other girls talking softly to one another down the hall. She glanced at her watch. It really *was* late. Mrs. Fogelman had said she would be back before the girls went to sleep. Why hadn't she come inside yet?

Kira was tucked into the daybed already, with Mary Rose on the pillow next to her. A few other dolls were gathered at her feet. The other girls had spread their sleeping bags out on the floor, and Tanya shot Maggie a look of gratitude when she noticed her own sleeping bag had been rolled out in the spot closest to the door. She heard the back door close below, and a moment later Mrs. Fogelman's clogs clomped up the steps. Tanya peeked her head out to wave, but the artist walked straight into her room without even a glance down the hall. She must have realized how late it was and figured the girls were already asleep.

The older girls slid into their sleeping bags. "Everyone's teeth are brushed?" Rebecca asked.

"Seriously, Becks?" Maggie said. "The whole *point* of a sleepover is to ditch our parents and forget about boring stuff like that. If I wanted someone to check on my oral hygiene, I could have just stayed at home!"

Kira giggled from her nest in the bed.

"Suit yourself," Rebecca said. "But oral health is very important. I brushed and flossed before I even put on my pajamas."

"You really are annoying, you know that?" Maggie asked.

"I try." Rebecca leaned back against her pillow with her hands behind her head, and Kira giggled harder.

The atmosphere was so festive that Tanya almost forgot why she had been afraid of the doll room in the first place. Clio yawned and stretched her arms overhead. "Okay, everybody, time for bed. I'm shutting off the light." She reached up and clicked off the lamp. The room was dark, but dim light from the hallway fell comfortingly across the girls sprawled on the floor.

Tanya could hear Kira rustling around in bed and she snuggled deeper under the covers. Rebecca and Clio whispered together for a minute or two before they, too, grew quiet. Next to her, Maggie sat up and flipped her pillow to the cool side before rolling over onto her usual stomach-down sleeping position. There was no other sound in the house, and Tanya lay awake listening to the others drift off to sleep around her. She slid her arm out of her sleeping bag and reached for her notebook and pencil, which she had tucked against the wall near her pillow. As her hand closed over the smooth, cardboard cover, she felt instantly more relaxed.

She pulled the notebook into the sleeping bag with her and unhooked the flashlight from her waistband, covering her head so the light wouldn't disturb the others. She didn't have anything in particular to record, but making notes always calmed her busy mind, and she hoped it would help her fall asleep. She wrote down the date and the time and popped her head out of her sleeping bag to peer at the window to see what the weather might be. The full moon peeked out from behind the clouds that crowded the sky, and Tanya watched the cotton-candy silhouettes drift across the silvery white disk. Tree branches moved in the wind, and a few stray leaves swirled up. The weather was changing.

Tanya recorded it all and paused, thinking about what else she wanted to add. Finally she wrote, *No further nightmares since the morning of the mirror burial.* It had been a relief to sleep soundly the past few nights. Of course, she hadn't been sleeping in a room full of creepy dolls, so she may have made that observation a bit too soon. She hoped not. Tanya slipped her notebook and pencil under her pillow and clicked off her flashlight. She curled into a tiny ball, and as she drifted off to sleep, she felt something nagging at the back of her mind. She ignored it, instead allowing the heavy pull of sleep to take over. But as her mind slipped into unconsciousness, she couldn't help but wonder if she was forgetting something. Something important.

CHAPTER
17

TANYA'S EYES FLEW open and she lay still, wondering what had awakened her. She took a moment to orient herself, letting her mind take inventory. Was it morning? No, it was still dark. Did she need the bathroom? No. Maybe a sound had awakened her? She listened, but she couldn't hear anything. She sat up and scanned the room. She could just make out the three lumps on the floor made by her sleeping friends and across the room the faint outline of Kira's head against the white pillow. The room seemed darker than it had been before. The moon had gone behind a cloud again, and the hall light was off. Tanya had no idea how long she'd been asleep.

She lay back down, but her eyes refused to close again. Something didn't feel right. Tanya wasn't the kind of person who believed in intuition, so she knew there must be some tiny detail that her subconscious mind had picked up on that her thinking brain had missed. It was weird that the hall light was off, but that wasn't enough to make her uneasy; Mrs. Fogelman could have turned it off after the girls went to sleep. What was it, then?

Her three friends were still on the floor beside her. Tanya's eyes had adjusted to the darkness now, and she sat up and looked again. Maggie was drooling onto her outstretched arm, her sleeping bag kicked halfway off and her red curls spread across the pillow. Rebecca lay on her side, her hands folded neatly under her cheek and a small smile on her face. She was probably dreaming about cupcakes. Clio was on her back, snoring gently. Her head was perfectly centered on her satin pillowcase, her hair a dark nimbus around her face. Kira was still cuddled up in bed.

But wait. Tanya looked closer. The shape of Kira's head looked strange. The little girl had a narrow, pinched face, and the shape on the pillow looked rounder. Tanya stood up in alarm. She remembered a story her mother told about her brother, Bryce. When he was three, he had had an allergic reaction to medicine, and his head had swelled up like a balloon. Was Kira having some kind of allergy attack? Tanya picked her way across the sleeping bodies. "Kira!" she whispered urgently. "Kira, are you okay?" There was no answer. "Kira," Tanya said louder.

Clio began to stir as Tanya reached the bed. "What's going on?" she mumbled, her voice fuzzy with sleep.

Tanya knelt on the floor by the bed and put her hand on Kira's forehead. She gasped in horror. It was ice cold. "Oh, no!" Tanya cried. "Kira?" She switched on the light and let out a tiny scream when she looked down. A large clown doll lay in Kira's place, its fat, round cheeks painted with bright red circles and its mouth stretched into a leering grin. The bell on its pointed hat jingled merrily as Tanya pushed it away in horror.

"What's wrong?" Rebecca asked, crawling out of her sleeping bag. Maggie sat up, too, her eyes still puffy with sleep.

"Kira's not in her bed," Tanya answered. She pointed at the clown doll. "This was in her place."

Rebecca blinked. "Okay. First rule of babysitting: don't panic." She stood up. "Maybe she's in the bathroom."

"I'll go check," Clio said. She disappeared but returned a moment later. "It's empty."

Rebecca chewed her thumbnail. "Maybe Kira woke up and decided that she wanted to sleep in her own room? I used to do that sometimes." She padded down the hall to investigate.

"Do you think she got scared and climbed into bed with her auntie Dot?" Maggie asked.

"Maybe," Tanya said. Rebecca came back into her room, and from her face Tanya knew she hadn't found Kira. "We have to spread out and find her," Tanya said.

"Has she ever sleepwalked?" Rebecca asked.

"I don't know, but I don't think so," Tanya answered. "At least not that anybody's ever mentioned." She switched on the hallway light and looked anxiously at Mrs. Fogelman's closed door at the end of the hall. Tanya would be embarrassed if she woke the older woman up to tell her that Kira was missing, only to discover the little girl was safe and sound in her great-aunt's room. "Let's try downstairs. Maybe she went to get a snack or something."

The girls quickly checked the rest of the upstairs, careful not to disturb Mrs. Fogelman yet. A search of the downstairs rooms proved fruitless as well, until Tanya heard Clio's cry of dismay. "What is it?"

"The back door's open!" The other girls found Clio in the sunroom, shivering by the open back door.

Tanya clicked on her flashlight. "Let's go. She can't have gotten very far."

Rebecca grabbed her arm. "Wait. We need coats and shoes. And grab an extra coat for Kira. If she's been sleepwalking outside, she'll be freezing." The girls rushed to the front hall and fumbled on their coats and shoes. "One of us should go wake Mrs. Fogelman," Rebecca said.

"I'll do it," Maggie volunteered. She ran back through the house and up the stairs.

The others piled out the back door, calling Kira's name. Somewhere in the neighborhood a dog barked, but otherwise there was no answer. Tanya swept the flashlight beam across the yard. "Why is it so dark?"

"The outdoor lights," Rebecca cried. "I'll go switch them on." A few moments later, the little lanterns along the path came on, but the rest of the yard lay in shadow. The lumpy shapes of Mrs. Fogelman's sculptures loomed, and it was impossible to tell what was what.

"Do you think she'd go into the studio?" Clio asked.

Tanya tried the door. "It's locked."

Maggie came running out the back door. "Kira's not in Mrs. Fogelman's room, either."

"Is she coming to help us search?" Tanya asked.

"I can't wake her up," Maggie answered. She shivered in the cold and zipped up her coat. Her eyes were large and frightened.

"You can't wake her up?" Rebecca repeated. "She's not . . . I mean, she's not, like, dead or anything, is she?"

"No," Maggie said. "She's alive and breathing. She's snoring, actually. But nothing I do seems to be able to wake her."

"We don't have time to worry about that now," Tanya said. "We have to find Kira." The balmy temperatures from the past few days had dropped dramatically, and there was a sharp bite in the air. The ground had hardened in the past few hours, and there was a fresh layer of frost that gave the grass a silvery cast as her flashlight beam swept across it. Wind rustled the tree branches and cut through Tanya's flannel pajama pants. She remembered the thin unicorn nightgown Kira had worn to bed. They needed to find her, and fast.

The clouds scudded across the sky, and bright moonlight lit up the yard. Clio pointed to a huddled figure near the old fish pond. "Over there!" The girls ran.

Kira stood in front of *Unburied Past*, Mary Rose clutched in her hands. Her feet were bare, and her stick-figure legs were marble white beneath the hem of her nightgown. Tanya threw a winter coat over the girl's thin shoulders. "Kira! Honey, are you all right?" She rubbed her hands briskly up and down

Kira's arms in an attempt to bring blood back into her frigid limbs. "Let's get inside where it's warm."

Kira didn't react. Instead, she continued staring into the depths of her great-aunt's sculpture. The dark arms of the pedestal reached up and twined around the basin encircling the gazing globe. Tanya could see Kira's thin face distorted and stretched in its milky reflection. Her eyes were hollow and blank, and her lips were turning blue.

"She may still be asleep," Rebecca said. "Let's get her inside and call my parents. They'll know what to do." She pried the doll from the little girl's arms and laid it on the ground beside her. With effort, the four of them were able to get Kira back inside and into the living room.

"I'll go get your phone," Maggie said. She ran upstairs.

Tanya switched on the gas fireplace and parked Kira in front of it. She knelt down and vigorously rubbed her hands along Kira's feet to bring the circulation back. Rebecca grabbed some blankets and wrapped them around the little girl. Clio sat next to Kira and began to warm her hands.

"Kira?" Tanya said. "Can you hear me?" Kira's eyes were blank, and she sat limply in the chair, pliant and unmoving.

Maggie came back down carrying four phones. She had a confused look on her face. "Rebecca, your phone's dead."

Rebecca looked up. "It is? But I plugged it into the wall charger before we went to sleep." She reached out one hand. "Can I use yours?"

Maggie swallowed. "All our phones are dead."

Rebecca stood up. "The house phone." She ran into the kitchen. She came back in a moment later. "It's dead, too."

Tanya looked out the window. "One of us will have to run for help. My house isn't far. We can go get my parents."

"I'll do it," Clio volunteered. She ran over to the front door and turned the deadbolt. She twisted the knob and yanked. It wouldn't budge. "I can't open it. There's another lock here, too, and it's the kind that needs a key," she called.

"Use the back door," Tanya called back. "The gate in the back fence should lead to the alley."

"I'll go with her," Rebecca said. The two girls rushed through the house to the back. When they returned a moment later, both girls were ashen. "The back door's locked now, too."

"What do you mean?" Tanya asked. "I don't think we even closed it behind us when we came inside."

"I . . . I don't know," Rebecca said.

"There has to be a set of keys somewhere," Clio offered. "Where does Mrs. Fogelman keep her purse?"

Tanya racked her brain, trying to remember. "The front closet," she said finally.

Clio opened the closet door and grabbed a tapestry bag that hung from a hook. "This one?"

"Yes," Tanya answered. She turned back to Kira. "Kira, can you hear me?" Kira didn't answer.

Clio rummaged frantically through the purse, but her hands came out empty. "They're not here."

"Mrs. Fogelman may keep them in her room," Maggie suggested. She stood up. "I'll go look for them and try to wake her again, too." She started up the stairs, but she stopped halfway up, and slowly backed down again, her face a mask of horror.

"What's wrong?" Tanya cried.

Maggie pointed wordlessly up the stairs.

Mary Rose sat at the top of the steps, the ring of keys in her lap.

CHAPTER 18

"H-HOW DID SHE get up there?" Rebecca asked, her voice barely above a whisper. "I left her outside."

From the top of the stairs came the tinkling laugh of a little girl. The sound trickled down Tanya's spine like ice. Mary Rose's face shone silvery-white in the moonlight, and her once-blue eyes now glimmered gold. She wore a long, black gown, and on her head was a doll-sized crown made of silver rams' horns.

Silver. The half-remembered thought that had been nagging at Tanya finally clicked into place. "The silver chest," she whispered aloud. "Of course. Everything in the Nightmare Realm is silver. Silver amplifies the queen's power; it doesn't neutralize it."

"But the paper that Ethan found," Clio said

desperately. "It was supposed to free Mary Rose from the Night Queen!"

Tanya shook her head. "'Freeing the vessel' wasn't about exorcising Mary Rose at all. It was about freeing the doll to do something bigger: prepare for the Night Queen's return."

Another giggle cascaded through the air like glass bells. Mary Rose stood. Her hands were empty; the keys had disappeared. She floated slowly down the steps, her blue-gold eyes glowing, her lips as red as blood against her snow-white face. When she spoke, her voice was high-pitched and light, like a small child's. "It is true. My return is certain now. There is but one final step." Her mouth stretched open, and Tanya could see jagged black teeth sprouting from her jaw. "The final vessel has been prepared." A spider leg burst from Mary Rose's skull, and then another. She had almost reached the bottom of the stairs.

Maggie shrunk against the wall. "What's happening to her?!"

Tanya didn't answer. She was frantically turning Mary Rose's words over in her mind. *Final vessel. Final vessel.* If it wasn't Mary Rose, then what was it? When she realized what it must be, her heart stopped.

Kira.

"It's Kira!" Tanya shouted. "Kira is the final vessel!" Tanya glanced over to the fireplace, where the little girl still sat limply in the chair, her face and limbs as slack and unresponsive as a doll's. For weeks the doll must have been draining her like a battery, preparing for the Night Queen's return. "We can't let Mary Rose take her!"

Mary Rose floated at the bottom of the stairs, her glowing eyes staring hatefully at Tanya. "What do we do?!" Maggie cried.

"There's four of us and one of her. We have to take her down!" Tanya lunged at Mary Rose, who floated away effortlessly with a tinkling laugh.

Clio was taller and managed to grab the doll's leg. Mary Rose struck like a viper. Her razor-sharp teeth slashed, and Clio fell back and clutched at her wounded arm. The girls were wary now and huddled together. Mary Rose's eyes gleamed with malignant glee. She licked her lips.

Rebecca grabbed a sofa cushion and swatted at the doll. One of her blows made contact, and Mary Rose tumbled against the wall. A china pinkie snapped off and fell to the floor. Another spider leg sprouted from her head, and Mary Rose drew closer to Kira. The other three girls tore the other pillows from the sofa and joined in, doing all they could to drive back the demonic doll. But Tanya knew it wasn't enough.

They didn't just need to slow Mary Rose down. They had to capture her and stop her for good.

Tanya found herself remembering a skittish runaway dog she had once found in the park. Nobody could coax it back to safety, until finally a neighbor had tossed a towel over the dog. Would the same thing work with Mary Rose? Tanya dropped her pillow and grabbed a thick, fleece blanket from a basket in the corner. "Try to knock her out of the air," she whispered in Clio's ear.

Clio leaped up and slammed the pillow into Mary Rose like she was acing a serve. The doll dropped like a stone, and Tanya threw the blanket on top, wrapping up Mary Rose as quickly as possible. The doll fought with surprising strength; its limbs felt like steel cables beneath the layers of wrapping. Tanya's arms, already weary from fighting it off, felt weak and trembly against the violent struggling of the blanket bundle. "I don't know if I can hold her."

"I got this," Maggie said. "She can't still bite, right?"

"There's, like, six layers of blankets between her mouth and anything else, so we should be pretty safe," Tanya answered.

"Good," Maggie said. She sat down on the bundle, and a muffled shriek of anger came from the folds. Tanya laughed in spite of herself. Everyone took a breath.

"So, what the heck just happened?" Rebecca asked.

"The paper that Ethan found. We thought it was an exorcism, but it wasn't. Instead, it was the next step to bringing the Night Queen back." Tanya shook her head. "I wouldn't be surprised if she somehow planted it there herself. None of us had ever seen it before, and it magically appeared at just the right moment for us to play into her hands."

"So, is Mary Rose the vessel, or is Kira?" Clio asked.

"I think Mary Rose was designed to be a temporary vessel for the Night Queen, but the doll is too small to contain her essence for long. She needs a living vessel in order to return to earth with her full power."

"Why Kira, though? Why not Mrs. Fogelman?" Maggie asked. "I mean, she had the doll for years. She said Mary Rose was like a daughter to her."

"I think Mrs. Fogelman's too old now," Tanya said thoughtfully. "The Night Queen needs children to feed her powers."

"But she can't do any of this without a beacon," Rebecca said. "And I thought we destroyed those."

"That's the part I don't understand," Tanya said. "Without the beacon, she can't fully return to our world. She can't make the change into Kira's body."

"Then why is she still trying?" Rebecca asked.

"I don't know," Tanya answered. "Maybe she

doesn't realize that there aren't any left. Or maybe she knows something we don't."

"So, what are we supposed to do now?" Maggie asked.

"I say we wait it out," Clio answered. "Whatever she thinks she's trying to do, she needed the full moon to act. If we can hold out until the sun rises, then her window of opportunity will close. All we have to do is make it through the night, and then we can destroy Mary Rose for good."

"Should we try to wake Mrs. Fogelman again? Maybe she can help us," Rebecca said.

Tanya shook her head. "I don't think we can. The Night Queen must have her under some kind of spell, like she does with Kira."

Maggie stole a glance at the chair by the fireplace. "What if destroying Mary Rose doesn't break the spell?" she asked in a whisper. "What if Kira and Mrs. Fogelman stay like this forever?"

"I didn't think of that," Clio said softly. "Maybe Ethan or Kawanna can find something that will bring her back."

"And this time I'll be more of a help," Tanya said. "If I had worked alongside Ethan, kept better notes, and vetted those sources, then maybe we wouldn't be in this mess." She picked at the dirt under her fingernails. "But I let my fear get in the way, and it made me sloppy." She shook her head. "Scientific procedures exist for a reason."

Rebecca grinned. "'Scientific procedures.' That's the Tanya I remember."

Clio's eyebrows arched. "Nobody's blaming Ethan because we got played by the Night Queen, are they? After all, it's not like any of us figured it out, either."

"Just friends, huh?" Maggie asked teasingly.

Clio frowned. She was just about to make a sharp retort when the lights went dark. The fire died in the hearth, and an ominous silence fell over the house. Even Mary Rose went still.

"I don't like this," Tanya whispered. The drapes at the window twitched, and there was a clatter from somewhere in the kitchen.

Something under the sofa cushions squirmed. A shadow darted out from beneath a chair, and Maggie let out a cry.

"What is it?" Rebecca cried. Tanya could see the wide whites of her friends' eyes in the faint light from the streetlamp outside.

There was another dark scuttle of movement from under the sofa, and Tanya felt a searing pain on her palm. She screamed and snatched her hand away from the floor. Similar yelps came from Clio and

Rebecca, and the girls pulled tighter together, searching for the unseen assailants.

There was a sound from upstairs. At first it was a kind of pattering. "Is that rain?" Clio asked softly.

"I don't think so," Rebecca whispered. The patter was joined by slithering scraping and then the pounding of something bumping down the stairs.

Not something. Lots of somethings. And they were headed to the living room.

From the hallway, a horde of dolls swarmed into the room like rats. The ones with firm-jointed bodies careened stiff-legged across the floor, and the soft-bodied rag dolls crawled, dragging their limp legs behind them. Their eyes were burning black suns, and jagged teeth crowded their mouths.

The girls jumped to their feet, their screams slicing the air. Tanya grabbed the struggling blanket bundle and held it over her head. "They're here to free Mary Rose! I'll keep them busy while you three protect Kira and try to find a way out!" Maggie and Tanya locked eyes, and Maggie nodded.

Maggie and Clio rushed to Kira and scooped her up between them while Rebecca worked to clear a path to the hall. Tanya heard Rebecca scream as a doll clamped its jaws around her ankle. She shook her leg free, and the doll hit the wall with a crack before

tumbling to the floor, only to stand up and advance again. Tanya paused in the kitchen doorway, torn. "Don't worry about us!" Rebecca shouted. "Just keep Mary Rose away from Kira!"

Tanya ran into the kitchen, the dolls right behind her. She jumped onto the counter, Mary Rose squirming in her arms. She stood up and held the heavy bundle as high overhead as she could. Within moments, the kitchen floor was teeming with tiny bodies struggling over one another and trying to gain purchase on the slippery tile floor. Her eyes searched the counter frantically, looking for something she could use to fight them off, but there was nothing.

Mary Rose's wriggling grew more aggressive, and Tanya's arms began to fail. The doll seemed to grow heavier by the second, and Tanya's fingers were numb from holding her arms up for so long. Down below, the dolls were beginning to pile up on one another, creating mounds the others could climb. They had almost reached the edge of the counter. Tanya kicked at them, but there were just too many. They streamed across the counter top, jagged teeth bared for battle.

When they started crawling up her legs, Tanya tried to shake them off, but they clamped down with their sharp little jaws and held on. She could feel their cold limbs through the thin fabric of her pajama pants. Soon they had reached her waist, and one began to claw its way up her back like a crab. Her arms were trembling violently now, and she gritted her teeth to keep from screaming.

Tanya was still wearing her winter coat, and when one doll began working its way up her sleeve, Tanya knew she was lost. Moments later, she was covered completely, and she fell to her knees. She felt razor-sharp teeth at her throat, and Mary Rose was pulled from her arms. Tanya watched in horror as the dolls reverently unrolled the blanket bundle and the demonic doll arose again.

Something had happened to Mary Rose while she had been cocooned in the blanket. Her face had begun to pit and crack, and a kind of sickly, gray light was radiating from the tiny openings. From outside the kitchen window, Tanya could see the same gray light streaming out from something in the yard. What could it be?

Tanya felt her arms pulled sharply behind her and tied behind her back. Mary Rose floated into the air, the cold gray light beaming from her cracked features. "Prepare the vessel now, my children. The beacon awaits us," she said in her high, breathless voice. "Bind the other mortals tightly. I have been waiting a long time for my revenge, and once I have returned to my true form, I shall enjoy seeing their bones ground to dust."

A river of dolls streamed into the living room, and Tanya could hear the screams of her friends as they tried to fight them off. She felt crawling dolls swarm over her, and for a moment she found herself staring into a golden pair of falcon eyes before everything went black.

CHAPTER
19

TANYA AWOKE TO find herself tied to a tree in the backyard, her shivering friends beside her. Each girl had cuts and scratch marks from trying to fight off the dolls, and all three were hunched over in defeat. Rebecca's teeth were chattering from the cold. "I'm sorry," she said. "We tried."

"I know," Tanya answered. "Me too. There were just too many of them."

"I still don't understand how this can be happening," Rebecca said. "I thought there weren't any more beacons left."

"There must have been another one we didn't know about." Tanya angled her head over to the line of dolls that marched toward the gray glow in the yard.

"Look." The glow was coming from Mrs. Fogelman's sculpture, *Unburied Past*.

"*Mrs. Fogelman* made the beacon?" Clio asked. "But how? Why?"

Tanya thought back to the feverish intensity of the artist's creative energy, the way she seemed to ignore everything else. The way her drive to complete the work seemed to come from somewhere outside of her. "I don't think she meant to do it," Tanya said slowly. "I think the Night Queen found some way to control or possess her, too. Just like she did with the people who made the other beacons we destroyed."

Maggie tugged against her bonds. "The Night Queen has Kira and the beacon. Once she fully enters our world, she'll destroy everything and turn the earth into another Nightmare Realm. There's nothing to stop her now, is there?"

"Nothing but us," Rebecca said. "Maybe we can find a way to free each other." She strained against the ropes around her wrists, trying to reach Clio's hands next to her. She twisted and squirmed, but she couldn't quite reach. "It's no use," she said.

Across the yard, a sea of dolls surrounded *Unburied Past*, and Mary Rose hovered above it, her crown gleaming in the unearthly light. A chunk of her china scalp fell to the ground as two more spider legs

punched through. Kira was slowly being led across the yard. She wore a long, ivory dress and a necklace of jet-black beads. Her eyes glowed with a dull gray light, and her lank hair had begun to rise up and stand on end.

"Look at her hair," Tanya said. "There's some kind of electrical charge between Kira and the beacon." Her hands itched to write down everything she was seeing, and she longed for her notebook, forgotten upstairs next to her pillow. If only she had it now, she might be able to make sense of it all, find some way to stop this from happening.

Kira shuffled closer to the beacon, her bare feet dragging across the frozen ground like a sleepwalker's. A sense of despair filled Tanya so deeply that it felt as if all her muscles had turned to lead. Suddenly, she jumped as something cold and slimy slithered between her arm and Rebecca's. Tanya let out a scream, and a cold, spongy hand clapped over her mouth. The pungent smell of decay filled her nostrils, and her eyes widened when a familiar face filled her vision.

It was the changeling, Horrible. The Night Queen's former servant was still an unreliable ally, but he did have a habit of showing up whenever they needed him most.

Tanya looked into his sunken-apple face and

nodded her understanding. Nimble fingers brushed against her wrists, and a few moments later, she and Rebecca were rubbing their cold hands together and waiting for Horrible to untie the other two girls.

"Horrible, where did you come from?" Rebecca whispered. "I thought you had left Piper weeks ago." The changeling finished untying the last of Maggie's bonds and waddled over to Rebecca on his bowlegs, the talons on his feet leaving divots in the frosty ground. He climbed into her lap and ran his mushroom-tipped fingers over her hair, grooming her. He picked out a stray piece of rotten leaf, and it disappeared into his mouth.

"Horrible, I'm glad to see you, too, but could you take this whole disgusto thing down a notch?" Maggie quipped with a grimace. "Or at least change your clothes every once in a while?" She pointed at the torn blue onesie that was streaked with filth, the same one he had been wearing when they first discovered him months earlier.

The glow from the beacon grew stronger, and Mary Rose's whole body was buzzing with energy. Another chunk of cheek broke off and fell onto frozen mud below. "I think we're running out of time," Clio whispered. "We have to find a way to stop her."

Tanya closed her eyes for a moment, picturing her

notebook. She mentally turned the pages, scanning through the notes in her memory. Even the supernatural world had rules. Rules that were governed by science, just like everything else. She thought back through what she had learned about elements. *Gold. Iron. Mercury.* She blinked and squinted, searching the scene before her. If the sculpture was a beacon, it had to follow the same rules as the other beacons. Something in it must have mercury, and if she could find it, she could destroy it.

Kira had almost reached the sculpture now, and Tanya could see the eagerness in Mary Rose's golden eyes. The Night Queen's triumphant return was close enough to taste. The gazing globe in *Unburied Past* roiled, and Tanya recognized the familiar oily sheen of the glass. Mercury glass.

Tanya knew she had only seconds to act. Without thinking, she grabbed the snow shovel by the back door. "What are you doing?!" Rebecca asked.

"Destroying the beacon," Tanya answered. She held the shovel in both hands, ready to swing.

"But that thing is cement," Maggie cried. "A shovel isn't going to be strong enough!"

"The beacon isn't the sculpture," Tanya said. "It's *in* the sculpture! It's the gazing globe!"

"What are you talking about?" Clio asked.

"It's *mercury* glass!" Without stopping to explain, Tanya ran straight for the sculpture. Just beside it, Mary Rose was bent over Kira, and a beam of bilious gray light was just beginning to come out of her mouth.

Tanya used the shovel to scoop the dolls in her path and fling them to the side. Several of the porcelain ones hit the wall of the studio and shattered, but the cloth dolls kept coming. Tanya knocked them away. With the flat end of the shovel, she swatted Mary Rose out of the air. The doll flew across the yard and slammed against a tree. Behind her, Tanya's friends picked up brooms, pots, and anything they could find to fight off the other dolls. "We've got to get to Kira!" Rebecca cried to the others.

There was a scream near the tree as a doll latched onto Maggie's arm. She desperately tried to shake it off. Clio knocked it away with a broom and stomped on its china head, crushing it. Dolls tore at Horrible, who seemed impervious to their bites. He plucked a rag doll from his leg and tore it in two. It fell limp to the ground at his feet.

Horrible mowed a path through the horde of snapping jaws, but the remaining ones closed ranks around Kira, some almost as tall as Tanya's waist.

Tanya turned back to the beacon. There, in the center of the basin, the gazing globe glowed the putrid color of filthy snow, its milky surface roiling with power. She stepped forward and raised the shovel over her head.

Just then, the clown doll appeared, blocking her path. Its jagged, yellow teeth dripped with a venomous liquid. Mary Rose loomed up behind it, her cracked and pitted face unrecognizable. Spider legs burst from every part of her like tentacles, and her black teeth jutted like knives beneath her golden falcon eyes. She vibrated with a white-hot energy. Tanya's heart froze in her chest like a mouse that has seen the shadow of the hawk above it.

"It is too late," Mary Rose intoned. Her voice had lost its breathless, childlike quality. There was a shrill note to it, almost one of desperation. Tanya could feel the searing heat coming off the doll. As Mary Rose closed in on her, Tanya noticed the clown's plastic face growing shiny. It softened and began to melt. The clown's brightly colored costume burst into flames.

Tanya used the shovel to fling the burning doll aside, praying the frost on the frozen ground would keep the fire from spreading further. The heat from Mary Rose was so great that Tanya could feel the shovel grow hot in her hands. She raised it over her head just as she felt blisters begin to form on her palms from the searing metal.

She slammed the edge of the shovel down on the gazing globe with all her might, and a spiderweb of cracks formed on its surface. Mary Rose screamed in fury, and Tanya heard another scream as Kira fell to her knees, clutching her head in her thin hands. The other dolls pushed Kira toward Mary Rose, who was still desperately trying to complete the Night Queen's final transfer into the little girl. Tanya raised her arms again, and this time the blow rang true. The globe shattered, the pieces catching the setting moon's glow as they flew into the night sky like fireworks.

Kira let out a keening wail and collapsed facedown into the dirt. Mary Rose's scream of rage shook the ground like an earthquake. Tanya dropped the burning hot shovel, her blistered hands an angry red. She fell to her knees and covered her face as Mary Rose flew at her, but before the doll could reach her, it exploded. Porcelain and cotton limbs sailed across the yard and burst into flames. The head and torso dropped to the ground, and the maw of a mouth opened, but no words came out. Only a final, fading hiss. The other dolls fell limp where they stood, arms and legs twisted at awkward angles, and their blank faces stared lifelessly at the frigid, early-morning sky.

Mary Rose's fiery form burned rapidly until all

that remained was a charred patch on the ground and a blackened silver lump in the shape of a tiny human heart.

Maggie hugged herself, wincing at the cuts on her arms. "What just happened? Is it over?"

Tanya took a deep, exhausted breath. "Yeah, it's over."

Clio knelt over Kira, who let out a moan and rolled over. The little girl blinked her pale eyes. "Where am I?" she asked blearily.

Tanya crawled over to her and helped her sit up. "You're outside in the yard," she said softly. "Do you remember how you got here?"

"I don't know," Kira said faintly. "I just remember that I was scared."

"I was scared, too," Tanya answered.

Kira slipped her hand in Tanya's. "But when I saw you, I felt better." She nestled her head against Tanya's arm. Tanya's eyes were suddenly damp, and she blinked and looked up to find Maggie beaming at her.

"Kira? Kira, where are you?" Mrs. Fogelman's sharp voice called out from inside the house.

Rebecca ran to the open back door. "We're out here!" she called inside.

The artist shuffled into the doorway wrapped in a red-and-black batik-print robe. She stepped into a pair of garden clogs and brushed her wiry curls back from her face. "What's going on?! It's not even the crack of dawn yet. Why is everyone outside?"

"We were looking for Kira," Tanya admitted.

Kira's face darkened. "I had a bad dream. It was about Mary Rose," she said sourly. "I hate that horrible doll, and I never want to see her again."

For the first time, Mrs. Fogelman looked around the rest of the yard, and as her eyes took in the sea of twisted, dismembered dolls, the charred patch of earth, and the shattered gazing globe, a flicker of understanding crossed her face. "Poor Kira must have been sleepwalking again."

"Um, yeah, I guess so," Tanya said, looking at the others.

"Much of my childhood is lost to me now, but I believe I used to sleepwalk quite a bit myself when I was Kira's age." Mrs. Fogelman looked down at the silver heart and the lone doll shoe that sat nearby, and her voice grew sad. "Mary Rose is gone, then?"

"I'm sorry," Tanya said. "We couldn't save her."

"It's probably for the best," Mrs. Fogelman said. "I don't think she was the right sort of doll for a little girl after all."

Kira burst into tears, and Mrs. Fogelman bent down and gathered her great-niece tenderly into her arms. Kira let out a long, keening wail. "I miss my mama," she cried, her body wracked with sobs.

Mrs. Fogelman, her face a mask of pain, rocked the little girl and stroked her hair. "I know, baby, I know. Auntie Dot is here for you, my love." Tears streamed down her face. "Something had ahold of me for a while, and I know I haven't been myself." She looked over at Tanya and her friends. "But I promise you, I'm here now."

CHAPTER 20

LATER THE NEXT day, the girls were settled around the little kitchen table in Kawanna's apartment while Kawanna and Ethan bustled busily about them, serving up pastries and tea. Tanya's bandaged hands were still tender, so she wrapped her palms gingerly around the teacup Ethan handed her, wincing a bit from the heat of the liquid inside it.

"Have you talked to Mrs. Fogelman since yesterday?" Maggie asked Tanya. "How's Kira?"

"She seems to be okay," Tanya answered. "Her great-aunt says she's eating and sleeping well, and her eyes are bright again. She doesn't seem to remember much."

"That's probably good," Clio said. "But what does Mrs. Fogelman remember?"

"More than most adults," Tanya said. "A lot of details are fuzzy for her, but she seems to know that she was possessed by something, and she wasn't very surprised to find her entire doll collection in pieces all over the backyard."

"What did she do with them all?" Maggie asked.

"Got rid of them," Tanya said. "Straight to the dump."

Maggie shuddered. "Good." She pulled up her shirtsleeve and eyed the scratch on her arm critically. "Do you think I'll get a scar?" she asked.

"I doubt it," Rebecca answered. "None of the cuts were very deep."

"Too bad," Maggie said wistfully. "Not many people could say they got a scar from fighting off homicidal dolls."

"True," Rebecca answered. "We are part of a very exclusive group."

Maggie's mouth quirked to one side, and she held up both hands for high fives. "Doll-bite sisters for life?"

The other girls laughed and slapped hands. "Doll-bite sisters for life!"

"So you won, right?" Ethan asked. "You beat the Night Queen."

"Yeah, and no thanks to you," Tanya retorted

jokingly. "It turns out your magic fix-it trick to exorcise Mary Rose actually just made her stronger." She shook her head in mock disappointment. "Honestly, Ethan, I expected more from you."

Ethan blushed and scratched the back of his neck. "Yeah, sorry about that. I guess I should have known that finding that paper at just the right moment might have been a little too good to be true."

"I'm just giving you a hard time," Tanya said. She put down her teacup and picked up a still-warm chocolate chip cookie from the platter in the middle of the table. "We all thought it was real. And besides," she added, "I'm the one who really put everyone in danger. I cut my fingers on those shards and started all of this. And when I felt like something was wrong, I just chalked it up to my own anxiety instead of listening to my intuition and taking it seriously. I didn't think scientists needed intuition, but I was wrong."

"Everyone makes mistakes," Kawanna said. "That's how we learn and get better."

"Well, I cut it pretty close." Tanya took a sip of her tea. "When all of you wanted to destroy the doll right away, I wouldn't do it. If I had just listened to everyone, maybe this whole thing could have been avoided." Tanya pulled Mary Rose's silver heart out of her pocket and held it up. "See this?" She shook it, and liquid could be heard moving around inside. "I'm pretty sure that's mercury in there." She put it down on the table. "Kira would never have had a chance as long as Mary Rose was around. You all were right."

Rebecca picked up the heart and tentatively ran her fingers over the realistic ridges and bumps in it. "What should we do with it? Bury it with the pieces of mirror?"

Tanya shook her head. "Liquid mercury is really poisonous, so this little sucker is going straight to the hazardous waste disposal center."

"Sounds like a plan to me," Kawanna said.

Tanya looked around the room, and her voice grew soft. "I just want to thank you for being there when I was scared and didn't know what to do. You were brave when I couldn't be, and you helped remind me of who I was when I needed it." She bent her head and picked at the hole in her jeans. "I'm pretty sure I'd be a total mess if it weren't for all of you."

"I think we'd all be total messes without each other," Clio said. "At least I would. Because I really, really hate fighting supernatural undead things. But if I *have* to fight a bunch of supernatural undead things, there's no one I'd rather do it with."

"You took the words right out of my mouth," Maggie said.

Rebecca rested her head on Maggie's shoulder. "Same."

Ethan reached for a peanut butter cookie. "So, what now?" he asked. "Is the Night Queen back in the Nightmare Realm, spying and waiting for revenge like always?"

"No," Tanya said. "Remember what Miss Pearl wrote about the vessel? How without the beacon it was doomed to wander and could never return home? Once we smashed the globe, the Night Queen was trapped in Mary Rose, and the doll just wasn't strong enough to hold that immense power. I realized it when I saw that it was starting to fall apart."

"I don't get it," Maggie said.

Tanya struggled to find a way to explain. "Imagine trying to fill a water balloon with a fire hose. Mary Rose was the balloon, and the Night Queen was the fire hose."

"Ohhh," Maggie said. "I think I get it." She bit her lip. "Kind of."

"The Night Queen was destroyed by her own power," Clio said thoughtfully. "She burned herself out."

"So, that's it, then?" Maggie asked. "We're done? No more supernatural battles?"

"It seems like it," Kawanna answered.

"It's about time for life to get normal again," Maggie said. "Because I've been seriously neglecting my wardrobe, Clio hasn't finished reading a book in months, and I don't remember the last time Tanya updated us on her Space Camp application." She took a bite of her cookie. "And no offense, Rebecca, but these cookies aren't exactly your best."

"Hey!" Rebecca laughed and tossed her balled-up napkin at Maggie.

Kawanna held up her teacup. "Sounds like it's time for a toast." The others held up their cups. "To normal life," Kawanna said.

"To normal life," they repeated, clinking their cups.

"And," Tanya said, holding her cup higher, "to friendship."

They clinked their cups again. "To friendship."

Outside the window, the last rays of the setting sun bathed the town in a warm amber glow, and deep purple shadows pooled behind the old buildings along Coffin Street. Piper, Oregon, was quiet once more. Its dark past had finally found peace.

EPILOGUE

BENEATH THE ARBOR of cobweb-draped trees, the dais sat empty and unswept. Piles of rotting red leaves lay in mounds that stained the stone below. The marble tombstone throne was pitted and streaked with moss, the carvings worn almost smooth from years of wear. The bonfire was cold and unlit, the embers damp from the dew that covered the glade. A tarnished silver crown of rams' horns lay forgotten in the weeds, left behind like a child's plaything.

The clearing was empty. No creature—living or dead—stirred between the thick trees. Even the babbling brook had dried up; only a few scum-laden puddles remained between the roots of the massive yew tree that stood, dead and broken, at the forest's edge.

The air was hushed and stagnant. No breeze stirred

the remaining few leaves of the twisted maple trees. Bare black branches stretched silently to the empty sky.

Then something rippled across the mossy ground. Sticks and stones danced as the earth began to shake. A dark crack split the clearing, black light oozing out of it like smoke. Something twisted and ancient rose from the inky black depths; darkness flowed out of it and curled across the ground like mist.

When the mist reached the trees, the trunks bent, cringing against the ground. The leaves on the dais turned black and swept away. A skeletal hand curled around the crown, and the metal bent and twisted itself into long, jagged spikes woven through with serpents.

The voice spoke with the rattle of dry branches scraping across a broken window. The rusty squeal of a forgotten door. The cold finality of soil dropped into an open grave.

"Yesssss," it hissed. "At lasssst . . ."

Acknowledgments

I've been traveling a lot this past year to promote my books, and one of the questions I get asked most often in my school visits is "Where do you get your ideas?" Some kernel of each idea usually comes from somewhere in my own life, and *The Vampire Doll* is no exception. Growing up, I was a stuffed animal person (still am), but my mother had two musty trunks where she kept her childhood doll collection. Her chipped and cloudy-eyed charges were the perfect combination of well loved and deliciously eerie, and on very special occasions I got to take them out and play with them. They have captured my imagination ever since.

Being on the road is exciting, but it's also tough. There were mornings when I would wake up and try to remember what day it was and what city I was in, and I am so grateful to all who made me feel at home no matter where I was. Jenny and Chris; Jason and

Jerry; Lori and Bob; Brenda and John; Claire; Danielle and Mark; Elly and James; Neville and Craig; and Regan and Mike are just some of the many wonderful people who hosted me this year and treated me like family. And special thanks to Alex Manfredonia, Jessica Myles Henkin, and Brendan Greeley for making my hometown always feel like home to me.

Enormous thanks to my parents for their continued enthusiasm and support. Through thick and thin, they still manage to cheer me on, check in on me, and affectionately strong-arm their friends into buying my books. My technophobe mother even managed to write an Amazon review. (And if you haven't written one yet, please do; they really make a difference!) Thanks also to Dallas and Amy Knudson, their kids, and my whole extended family of in-laws and out-laws for your good humor and willingness to show up, especially when I need it most. (I'm looking at you, Matthew Gamarra!) I love each and every one of you.

Children's book people are some of the best people around, and I'm so lucky for all the book people that made this work such a joy. Erin Stein, Nicole Otto, Weslie Turner, and the wonderful team at Imprint are just so cool and smart, as are Katie Halata, Kelsey Marrujo, and the many other terrific publishing folks

I've had the pleasure of working with on this series. Even in a big house like Macmillan, they always make me feel like I matter. Illustrator Rayanne Vieira has been a joyful collaborator, and I loved seeing how she brought these characters to life in each book. My incomparable agent, Erin Murphy, and beloved extended EMLA family continue to nurture and sustain my creative spirit, as do the wonderful Minnesota and SCBWI writing communities. And extra special thanks to all the teachers, librarians, and other champions of children's literature who work every day to connect kids to books they will love.

I am profoundly grateful to my husband, Eddie Gamarra, for the incredible love and encouragement he has shown me throughout every moment of my writing career. He has supported my work as an author financially, emotionally, and creatively, and he has planned unbelievable surprises and thoughtful gestures to mark each special milestone along the way. None of these books could have been written without him. What a remarkable gift it has been to have him by my side.

For me, the heart of this series has always been the friendship between the girls, and the way they accept and support one another in all of their messiness and mistakes and imperfections. Because that is what friends do. I am not an easy friend to have, and for all who have embraced me wholeheartedly, loved me when I felt unlovable, and allowed me to fail and try again, there are no words I can possibly string together that can adequately express my thanks. Whether I've known you for forty years or forty minutes, my life is richer with you in it. Your love is the very air I breathe, and my gratitude for each of you knows no bounds. Thank you, dearest ones. Thank you all.

About the Author

KAT SHEPHERD loves to create fast-paced adventure stories that are likely to engage reluctant readers, because she wholeheartedly believes that reading should be a joyful experience for every child.

A former classroom teacher, Kat has also spent various points in her life working as a deli waitress, a Hollywood script reader, and a dog trainer for film and TV. She lives in Minneapolis with her husband, two dogs, and a rotating series of foster dogs. Babysitting Nightmares is her first middle grade series.

katshepherd.com

babysittingnightmares.com